"I'm only in town for a year...."

"Not much time to get acquainted with you before I go back overseas." Jon moved his hand across the table toward hers and touched her fingers. "Would you consider finishing your studies in Europe?"

She laughed, secretly thrilled at his interest. "We haven't even had dinner, and you're already planning my future."

His banter matched hers. "Tobby, for the last hour, I have not been able to contemplate a future without you."

I will not blush, she thought. I will not let this stranger tease me. And yet, as she met his gaze, she could not be certain whether his words were an untrustworthy combination of flattery and flirtation. Or whether he indeed spoke the truth from his heart....

Books by Doris Elaine Fell

Love Inspired

Long-Awaited Wedding #62
The Wedding Jewel #74

DORIS ELAINE FELL

With books and dolls as her companions, Doris knew from the time she was seven that she wanted to be a nurse and a writer when she grew up. She also wanted to escape the confinement of a tiny home-town with a railroad track smack in the middle. Challenged by these childhood dreams and her first train ride to the Pacific Northwest, she pursued a multifaceted career as a teacher, missionary, nurse, freelance editor and author. Her diverse professions have taken her to a Carib village in Guatemala, a Swiss chalet in the Alps, around a rugged mountain road in Mexico and aboard an ocean liner across the Pacific to a bamboo schoolhouse in the Philippines. She also thoroughly enjoys her teddy bear collection and sitting by a river in eastern Washington with her great-nieces and great-nephews.

But it was as a high schooler that Doris knelt by her bedside and asked God for the privilege of one day writing for His glory. For the last nine years she has written full-time, thus fulfilling her writing dream and expressing her love for a gracious God and her love of life and living in her six-book SEASONS OF INTRIGUE series with Crossway Books and in her mainstream novel *Blue Mist on the Danube* for Fleming Revell. *The Wedding Jewel* is her second romance novel with Steeple Hill. The subtle theme of forgiveness marks her writing.

The Wedding Jewel
Doris Elaine Fell

Love Inspired®

Published by Steeple Hill Books™

STEEPLE HILL BOOKS

Steeple
Hill™

ISBN 0-373-87074-4

THE WEDDING JEWEL

Visit us at www.steeplehill.com

Printed in U.S.A.

But there is a friend
that sticketh closer than a brother.
                                    —*Proverbs* 18:24b

Now that same day
two of them were going to a village
called Emmaus, about seven miles from Jerusalem.
They were talking with each other about everything
that had happened. As they talked and discussed
these things with each other, Jesus himself
came up and walked along with them, but
they were kept from recognizing him.
                                    —*Luke* 24:13-16

IN MEMORY OF OUR JEWEL
WITH LOVE

Prologue

Home! Home to Auburn.

The town of Auburn was brilliant with the crimson reds and goldenrod yellows of early September. Tobin Lynne Michelson strolled carefree up the narrow street beneath the burnt-orange maple leaves and a pearl-blue sky. She savored being alone, savored the briskness of the day, the fresh scent of the air after last evening's rainfall. Ribbons of tiny rainbows reflected in the puddles on the sidewalk. Last week's Indian summer had faded, the fall rains begun.

Outwardly, Tobin looked as if she had not a worry in the world, stepping lightly as she did. Inwardly, she was beginning to feel overwhelmed, trapped. She had left Auburn five years ago, vowing never to come back again except for holidays and special family occasions. And here she was back in the old hometown for a year of graduate study. Still unmarried. Still shirking family responsibility, as her father would say.

She crossed the street at Elm and Bradshire and made her way up the main thoroughfare, past the familiar landmarks of her undergraduate days: Mrs. Tippins's candy store with its flower box of impatiens in front, the campus book mart that covered half a block and the Knightbridge Café where the students hung out on weekends and after class. Music and laughter blared through the open door. She smiled, wondering how she had ever endured the noise and crowd. The Knightbridge Café was the place where she and Kedrick had escaped the parsonage confinement and spent hours munching fish and chips and solving the problems of the world.

But they had never solved Kedrick's problems. Kedrick, her sullenly good-looking twin brother with so much going for him and so little accomplished. She was a mirrored reflection of Kedrick with her blue-green eyes and thick dark lashes, and in spite of his wayward ways, he had her undying loyalty. Kedrick, the reason she had come home.

Ahead of her she heard a car door slam and a deep masculine voice call, "Tobin!"

Startled, she looked up into the familiar face of an Auburn policeman. Dark curly hair. Shiny broad forehead. A freckled nose. A smile tugging at his full lips. She did a double take and came up with a name. The right one, she hoped. Brent Carlson.

"Brent. Hi. I didn't realize you were a man in blue."

"Signed up for the police academy the year you went away." He kept grinning. "Home on holiday?" he asked.

"I'm at the university."

"Again?"

She nodded. "I'm going for my master's."

"So you're still studying jellyfish and loggerhead turtles?"

"I'll be part of the Oceanographic Institute—the graduate school in marine biology."

"Wow! Not everyone gets in."

"I know. I'm glad I did."

"You've been gone a long time, Tobby."

"Just five years."

"I stop your mother now and then to check up on you."

"Not for speeding, I hope?"

He looked beyond her, avoiding her gaze. "Your brother's the one with speeding tickets and the DUIs."

Bits and pieces were coming back now. She had met Brent during her senior year at the university. Sat beside him in a class or two. Had banana splits with him at the café. She had thought him attentive, attractive, but a homespun boy. He had admired her dreams of being a marine biologist. She had marveled at his to live out his life in Auburn. They had been friends. Somewhere else, they could have been more.

"I've been following your career, Tobby. A naturalist at the state park. Your appointment at the aquarium. What's next?"

"A study program for the next three years."

His face brightened. "Then you've come home for good?"

"I'll go for my doctorate elsewhere. Then back to

the research work at the aquarium. Or on to something bigger and better.''

"You always had big dreams. I rarely leave the city limits except for a baseball game." He hooked one thumb on his belt. "Or when my squad car is in hot pursuit of a carjacker,''

"I thought Auburn was a quiet town. Drug free. No bank robberies.''

"We have our problems. Now tell me, where are you staying?''

She winced, not wanting to tell him. "At the parsonage.''

Back in my old corner bedroom that looks out on the university campus and town golf course and beyond to the cemetery.

"The parsonage?" It was his turn to laugh. "You're kidding. I thought you'd never stay there again.''

"The choice lodging was taken by the time I got here.''

His smile turned sympathetic. "You have to come early. We're dead in the summertime, but we have a population explosion every fall—Auburn about doubles when the school term opens.''

"I know, but my decision to come was a last-minute one.''

His gaze held steady and she wondered if he knew why she had come home. She flicked back a strand of her nut-brown hair and met his gaze. "A month ago I planned to go east to school.''

"A thousand miles away from Auburn?''

"At least that.''

She had applied to several universities across the country and been accepted by three of them. At the last minute she'd scuttled it all because her family needed her.

He drew her back, saying, "People are rezoning their homes so they can take in students. Something's bound to open up."

"I'm settled in now—another move wouldn't set well with my family. Sounds crazy coming from me, but I don't want to make waves. I'll just buck the crowds."

"That's what I'm doing, but I don't like it either—especially when they haven't increased the police force. It's the same old battle for law enforcement. Not enough funds."

"Brent, Auburn is peace loving. We'll do just fine."

"Yeah," he said without enthusiasm. "But you've come back to big time. The Oceanographic Institute has built a name for itself. That's part of the unexpected influx. And then—" he grinned "—we have a celebrity in town."

"Movie star?"

He pushed back his cap and scratched his forehead. "Nope. A famous foreign correspondent. Got his name in photojournalism."

"Really? Gramps hasn't said a word about that."

"He will. Can't remember the man's name offhand, but he built his reputation during the Gulf War and in Bosnia. Seems to me he covered the IRA conflict in Ireland, too."

"Well, it's doubtful our paths will cross '

The glint in Brent's eyes sharpened. "That's a good thing. I don't relish any competition where you're concerned."

He tapped the hood of his black-and-white, his ear cocked toward the radio static. "I still have a few minutes' break. How about coffee at Knightbridge's?"

Tobin glanced at her jeweled watch—eleven already. She was running late. And she couldn't risk Kedrick seeing her sipping coffee with a policeman.

"I'd better not. I'm on my way to the newspaper office. I'm hoping to have lunch with my grandfather."

Brent masked his disappointment. "Some other time then?"

"We'll see."

"Give old K. T. Reynolds my greetings."

"Drop by and give him your own greetings. He'd like that."

"I do sometimes. But it's usually over police business. But I read his editorials. The old man still has it. I hate to think of a time when he won't be running the paper."

"He wants my brother to take over."

"Not likely," Brent said soberly. "You'd be a better bet."

"I'm only here for a year, remember?"

He stepped back to let her go. She felt his eyes on her as she walked away, but she waited until she was out of Brent's vision before brushing away the tears that stung her eyes. Was she the only one who still believed in Kedrick?

What have I come home to? she wondered. She knew that Brent Carlson could be a fun person to be with, but she had no intention of starting a relationship with anyone in the old hometown. She was here for a year and that was it. Besides, it would never do to have a man in blue calling at the parsonage, even if it was only for a cup of coffee. Kedrick had already warned her. Policemen were not welcome at the Michelson house.

Chapter One

As she crossed Juniper to the *Auburn City Herald,* Tobin sensed a quickening of her spirit, a growing excitement. Once she had wanted to stay on and work her way up to the science editor's desk. But her fascination with nature and her need to study it firsthand won out.

Her grandfather's newspaper complex covered an entire city block. The main office was a mixture of the old and new—the ancient facade much as she remembered it from childhood, the renovations mostly inside. Even as she reached the curb she could see *Auburn City Herald* and the bold black words K. T. Reynolds, Publisher, clearly marked on the plate-glass windows that stretched across the front.

Tobin burst through the revolving glass doors into the bustling excitement of her grandfather's world. To keep the family business going, Gramps had gone modern. The remembered clacking of typewriters and

the old scent of newsprint had long ago vanished with
the installation of computer terminals.

It was all familiar—the rows of computer tables
and desks, the metal files being slammed shut, the
persistent ring of the telephones, the static of police
radios, the clatter of the wire services. She paused just
inside the city room to check the window display. It
rarely changed—framed headlines for the past hundred years, some of them back to her great-
grandfather's time. The section in the middle was always new. She studied the accompanying photos with
a practiced eye. They were outstanding images—the
somber faces of Omagh, Ireland, in black and white
by Jon Woodward, whoever he was.

She glanced around again, smiling at no one in par-
ticular. The science editor had two phones going at
once, his head cocked toward the massive wall clock
with its constant reminder of deadlines. Tobin had
spent numerous hours as a child nosing around the
office or hanging over the picture editor's desk when
she wasn't peeking around the clutter in her grandfather's cubicle and smiling up at him. The last three
years before she moved away she had been on staff
part-time as a budding reporter. Her gaze settled on
the receptionist. Becki Murdock had been with the
Herald almost as long as Tobin's grandfather.

"Miss Michelson," Becki called with pleasure.
"K.T. told us you were in town. Are you coming
back to work for us?"

"Can't. I'm studying full-time at the university."

Becki's smile faded. "But we need you on as a

staff photographer. You were always so good with the camera.''

"That's Kedrick's job. You don't need two Michelsons taking pics for the paper.''

Becki flushed. "We were hoping you were back to replace your brother.''

Before Tobin could answer, Tip Warren, the foreign editor, waved frantically. "Pint-size, get over here and give your old friend a hug.''

Tip pushed himself to his feet, met her halfway and pressed his bristly cheek against hers. She was back. She was welcomed. "You've grown a foot since the old days," he accused. "What brings you this way?''

"I'm looking for my brother and grandfather.''

"Haven't seen Kedrick at all today. And when he comes he doesn't see any need to punch in the time clock. But you know where to find old K.T. He's back in his cubicle.''

She pushed her way through a maze of computer desks, greeting old friends as she went, smiling shyly at the new reporters. Her grandfather's copy desk was at the other end of the room in a glass-enclosed cubicle, but she was so busy greeting everyone that she failed to glance inside.

She shoved open the door, a giant-size smile on her face. "Gramps, I'm here.''

A rangy stranger turned to face her. He looked thirtyish, an attractive man with an unruly lock of dark hair sweeping across his forehead. He stood by the bookcase, one of her grandfather's favorite black-and-white war photos in his hands.

Strong, suntanned hands. An onyx ring on his second finger. Her gaze strayed back to his face. She couldn't decide in that moment whether he was handsome or not, and decided he would definitely be noticed in a crowd. He had a most pleasant face—a firm jawbone, well-set eyes, even teeth. Thick brows arced as he watched her.

"Hi," he said.

In the confusion, the smile vanished from her face. "I—I'm sorry. I was looking for my grandfather."

"So I gathered." His voice was deep, and she found herself blushing under his unblinking gaze. "He's about somewhere. Can't be gone long."

She felt flustered, the stranger perfectly at ease. "You're new around here," she said.

A smile lit his hazel eyes. "I was going to tell you the same thing. But your grandfather warned me you were coming."

"Warned you? Then you know who I am."

"But not the name. Or at least I gathered the one he used was not your given name."

She couldn't imagine which nickname Gramps had used. Pipsqueak. Or doll. Or that's my gal. Or something worse. Embarrassed, she said, "I'm Tobin. Tobin Lynne Michelson."

He went on leaning against the bookcase, giving her a long appraisal. "I'm Jon. Jon Woodward."

She pointed back with her thumb. "Then you did those photographs out there in the newsroom. The ones on the faces of Ireland. Not bad work."

"Thank you," he said, amused. "And you are Tobin, the marine biologist? An unusual name, isn't it?"

She flicked a strand of hair behind her ear. "It's a family heirloom. And not unusual if you know my grandfather."

Jon chuckled, and she liked the warmth of his laughter. "Then explain the heirloom," he said.

"My grandfather had no sons. It grieved him to think his name would die with him, so Mother gave my brother, Kedrick, his first name and I ended up with his middle name, Tobin."

"The name Tobin fits you. It's special."

"I like it."

"Your grandfather and I have been getting acquainted these last few weeks. I've admired his work for a number of years and have been reading his editorials since moving to Auburn. I like a man who sets the tone for his paper with fairness and truth."

"Then you really know the heart of my grandfather. He's such an honest man, no matter what his critics say."

"A man like K. T. Reynolds will always have enemies, but I'm not one of them. I studied some of his photojournalism shots in college. He put a human face to the Korean War and the conflict in Vietnam. Many photographers learned from him. I know I did."

She felt touched that this stranger knew of her grandfather's work. It had been part of his past that she and Kedrick knew little about. He had come home after some time in Vietnam to take over the paper. And later, when Kedrick and Tobin came along, he put cameras in their hands and taught them how to catch the emotion, the heart of a person, through the eye of a camera lens.

"Gramps is hitting seventy-five. Did you know that?"

Jon whistled. "And he's still going strong."

"He won't quit. He wants to keep the *Herald* in top shape until my brother takes over."

"Is that likely, Tobin?"

"I don't know. So many people in Auburn think Gramps is nothing but a hard-nosed journalist—and an utter fool to try and groom his grandson for the job. But the paper has been in our family for generations. And Gramps made a success of it."

"But you're not sure your brother will?"

"I'm not certain what Kedrick really wants to do. That's one of the reasons I came home again. Kedrick is almost twenty-seven. We both are, but my parents think he will never grow up."

"Twins, then?"

She nodded. "But tell me, Jon. Do you work for the paper? Are you one of the new reporters?"

"No, he doesn't work for me," K. T. Reynolds shouted as he barreled into the room. "Can't even talk him into a few good photographs for the paper."

He paused long enough to kiss his granddaughter on the cheek before sinking into the swivel chair and swiping his snowy-white hair back with both hands. She hated it when people thought of him as a gruff old man. He was mellow as a kitten whenever she was around. For a second she grieved for him. What if Kedrick didn't take over the family business? What if the paper folded when her grandfather quit? No, he would never quit. Chances were he would turn up his toes and die right here where he had spent most of his life making a go of the *Herald*.

As he adjusted his hearing aid, he startled her, asking, "Where's that brother of yours, Tobby? He knows we have a paper to get out."

"I don't know. I was supposed to meet him down here and pick up my car. He borrowed it early this morning so he could get to work on time."

Gramps scowled. "What's wrong with his own wheels?"

"He said his van was in the shop again."

"With another bent fender? Don't be loaning him your car, Tobby. Let him walk." He glanced up at Woodward. "I see that you two have met."

"She even called me Gramps," Jon said, his eyes twinkling. "But I set her straight."

K.T. roared with laughter, his chuckle sounding like a tuba blast booming through the cubicle. "I wouldn't wish that off on anyone." But he winked at Tobin and she smiled back.

They had always been friends, buddies, and the thought of him one day not being there for her stirred an ache deep inside.

Jon put the framed photograph back on the shelf. "I think I'd better go. We'll talk again, sir. If I get any good shots for you, I'll bring them in. Let you look them over."

"Good luck on your classes, Woodward."

"So far they're going well. If they'd just assign me a lab assistant, it would even be better."

He was standing beside Tobin now, smiling down

at her. "I've enjoyed meeting you. Perhaps our paths will cross again soon."

"They will," Gramps said. "I'll make a point of it."

Woodward was just out of shouting distance when Gramps said, "Well, how do you like him?"

"Mr. Woodward?"

"You didn't meet anyone else, did you?"

Impishly she said, "Brent Carlson on my way down here."

"Forget Brent. Now, Jon—that's someone I enjoy. Nice to have a photographer of that caliber in town for a year."

"Should I recognize his name?"

"Probably not. He's been abroad for several years. Started out as a correspondent for the *London Times*. Moved on from there to cover the entire continent as a photojournalist." He shoved a stack of papers around his desk, hunting for something and not finding it. "I envy him. He's filmed royalty and wars and every major sporting event abroad. He's a good man, honey. No pretense. I like that about him." Gramps pushed his chair back and stood again, fingering the books on his shelf. "Here. This is one of Woodward's books."

He flipped the book open and tapped one of the faces. "That young man has heart. He knows people. You can see it in the expressions he captures."

"So what's he doing in Auburn?"

"Hiding out for a year. Teaching at the university. Can't believe we got a man like that," he repeated. "He was on hand for the embassy bombings in Africa and more recently that mess in Ireland. He came home six weeks ago on a sabbatical."

"Married?" she asked casually.

"No, and he's not looking. At least, that's what he told me. But then, he said that before he met you."

"Oh, Gramps."

"I'm just looking out for your best interests, honey."

"He might have been married," she said cautiously. "I'd have to know that before I'd take a second look."

She was teasing but suddenly she realized Jon Woodward *had* been appealing. Sharply dressed. Polite. Kind in his remarks about her grandfather. Why would someone like that—a successful man about the world, according to Gramps—still be single?

"I have a production meeting in five minutes, sweetie."

"Then I'm out of here, Gramps."

"You could stay and sit in on the meeting."

"And listen to you fuss at your staff."

"That's what you call it, eh? I'm running a newspaper around here. I expect the best and I get it. News is happening somewhere in this world of ours every second and I'm here to capture it for the people of Auburn."

"And to beat your competition."

"Around these parts I am the competition." His gravelly voice oozed with confidence. "Will I see you at dinner this evening?"

"You're coming to the parsonage tonight? But, Gramps, I was planning on going out with friends."

"Suit yourself, but you know your father and I need an arbitrator. Besides, your mother is cooking pot roast for Jon Woodward. Now get along," he said, as he had always said when she was a child. "And I'll see you at dinner."

Chapter Two

Tobin walked down Juniper in the noon sun, feeling increasingly peeved with her brother. He had borrowed her shiny new car to go to work, and here she was footing the mile and a half back to the parsonage in the heat of the day. She raced with the crowd toward Elm and Bradshire, but when she reached the Knightbridge Café she decided to endure the loud music and test whether the fish and chips were as good as they used to be.

Turning in her order at the counter, she found an empty booth by the window. She had just propped her elbows on the tabletop when a pleasant voice said, "May I join you?"

Jon Woodward dropped casually onto the wooden bench. "A noisy café," he said. "Would you like to go someplace else?"

"I've already ordered."

"Well, the food's good—and it gives you a fair view of the student body outside the classroom."

She cupped her ears. "I should apologize. The music is deafening."

"You forgot. I'm used to the sounds of a war." For a flash his eyes clouded, and then he was smiling again. "I was hoping you'd come by here on the way home."

"A chance in a million."

"It was worth taking. I called the newspaper office on my pager and told the receptionist it was an emergency."

She shook her head. "Becki Murdock is a hard one to convince. She protects my grandfather—screens all his calls."

"She put me right through to the conference room."

"Bet that didn't set well with my grandfather."

"He took it well. We have an understanding. He wants me to do some photos for the paper, so he told me to try the café."

"Gramps said you're teaching at the university."

"You can call it that. I got in on my experience, not my teaching credentials. I've been one of those roving photojournalists for most of my life."

"You make yourself sound ancient."

"Does thirty-four qualify?" His brow arced. "It didn't hurt my cause any when the previous instructor quit at the last minute."

"Is your family here in Auburn with you?"

"I'm alone—if you can call living in a boarding-house on Maple living alone. I have the attic room to myself. That comes with breakfast privileges and dinner, provided I'm there on time. Miss the six p.m. deadline and you're out."

Her thoughts raced. Alone in Auburn. But are you married? Separated? Widowed? she wondered. Was there ever someone special in your life? Was there ever anyone special in her own?

Tobin felt vulnerable under his steady gaze, as though he were homing in on her features through a camera lens—as though he were reading her thoughts.

"You'd make a good model. I could use you in my classroom."

Her immediate impression was a sheet-draped model on a high stool with her long legs crossed and her bare feet dangling. As she felt her cheeks blotch, she considered walking off and forgetting her lunch.

"This week I want to teach my students about angling in on a face—catching impromptu photos. Catching the person. Seeing their eyes. Feeling their heart. I want them to see their subject the way you are right now. Fresh and alert. Natural. You've got a great complexion even with your rosy cheeks."

He leaned forward, all but tilting her chin as he studied her. "I want them to realize if they photographed you at just the right angle, they'd catch the dimple in your cheeks. Those wide questioning eyes. The perplexity on your brow."

She kept staring at him, wondering whether he was for real.

"Tilt your head to the side," he said. "There. Just like that. You're very expressive, Miss Michelson. Very lovely."

He hesitated for a moment. "Do you always wear your hair that way? Swept back from your face?"

That's how she had combed it—swept back and leaving her with a shiny broad forehead. Had she used her powder? She couldn't remember. She had been in a hurry this morning, brushing her long hair to a shine and then whipping it back from her face and twisting it into a high coil. She wished now that she had let it hang freely, softly around her face. That way the sun would catch the nut-brown gleam that was the envy of her friends.

"What do you say? Will you come and be my model?"

She repressed her excitement. "Outside or in the classroom?"

"In class on Monday and Tuesday. Then I'll send my class out on their own, cameras in hand. I want them to stroll through the campus and get candid shots. Or go over to the city park and catch the expressions on the elderly just sitting there, or the children playing."

The waitress arrived with Tobin's fish and chips and tartar sauce. She moved her arms to make room. "Looks good," she said.

"So do you, Tobin. So will you help me out?"

"I'll think about it."

He sighed. "If not, I'll use one of the students. I'm certain my friend Jade Wellington would help me."

The name sounded familiar to her but she couldn't place it.

"She's as Scandinavian-looking as they come— high cheekbones and sea-blue eyes"

"You don't miss much." She felt a bit deflated. She should have known a man as attractive as Jon would not be lacking for young women eager to help him out.

"The truth is, I'd like to use both of you. There's something of contentment in your face. Confidence. Beauty. With Miss Wellington, there's a sadness that her chuckle and mischievous grin and beauty can't hide. You'd be a study in contrast."

"You're trying to expose how we feel inside?"

He nodded. "That's right. It took me years to learn it. I have at least a hundred and twenty students in my classes. I'll be lucky if four or five of them learn to focus their camera lens on the face in the crowd. I want them to catch the heart, the pain, the dreams of that person."

He sounded as committed to photojournalism as she was to biology. But something frightened her. If he focused his camera on her right now, he would see her heart and know that it was beating unusually fast in his presence.

As he finished his second cup of coffee, he relaxed. "I enjoyed meeting your grandfather. I have family friends living in Auburn now, but your grandfather is the reason I moved here for the year. He had great potential—could have gone on to make a name for himself in photography. One of the greats."

"He's well-known in this area."

"But he could have been known worldwide. I've always wanted to meet K. T. Reynolds—a man who gave up a promising career as a photographer to take over the family business. But it plunged him into oblivion."

"And you want to slip into oblivion here in Auburn?"

"I just want some of his strength of character to rub off on me. Under that gruff exterior I see an honest man. A happy man."

"And after this year, will you settle in the States?"

"No. I'll go back to Europe. There will still be wars to cover. And sporting events. And the human side of people."

Tobin hated it when her heart raced out of control as it was doing now. She had known Jon Woodward all of three hours and found herself liking him more and more. She had seen his photos of the somber faces of Omagh and flipped through one of his books of black-and-white photos. She liked his work; her grandfather admired it. Now she was getting a glimpse—slightly out of focus, perhaps—of the man behind those pictures. His mask was one of pleasantry, of charm; her grandfather's a gruff exterior. But the two men were alike. Both caring. Both gifted.

She pushed her plate away and glanced at Jon Woodward and liked what she saw. In the sunlight that streamed through the café window, she noticed flecks of green in those sensitive hazel eyes. The top button of his sports shirt lay open, his neck muscled and thick. In someone else she would have disliked the unruly strands of dark hair that tumbled over his forehead. In Jon Woodward, it made him boyish, charming.

"Do I pass inspection?" he asked.

Her cheeks warmed again with color. "I was just studying you through my camera lens—to see whether you'd pass the test in your own classroom."

"And do I?"

"You're the instructor. What do you think?"

He seemed perfectly at ease as he watched her. "Tobin, this is the first enjoyable day I've had since reaching Auburn."

"You don't like it here?"

"I like it. But I'm a free spirit, and here I am night after night trying to figure out how to challenge one hundred and twenty students who thought my class would be a breeze or little more than the click of a camera."

"You'll do all right," she said. "I know my grandfather will help you if you need his expertise."

"You're fond of your grandfather. I like that about you."

"We've always been friends. I can't remember a time when he wasn't there for me."

The thought caught midcycle. A lump welled in her throat. For the second time this morning she allowed herself to dread the time when he wouldn't be there, when she wouldn't have him to lean on. "Sounds childish—me being almost twenty-seven."

His dancing eyes seemed to say, *Twenty-seven. Merely a child.* Aloud he said, "Not childish at all. Very mature. I lost out on the grandparent generation. My parents married late in life. I came along even later. I don't have them any longer."

"I'm sorry."

"Nothing to be sorry about. We had good years

together. I still have an older brother and sister. We keep in touch.''

"I just have Kedrick," she said thoughtfully. "No sisters. Kedrick and I lived at the *Herald* when we were kids. That noisy old place was our favorite playground."

"Where were your parents, Tobin?"

"They were busy running the church—Dad in the pulpit and Mom heading committees and organizing potluck suppers. She adores Dad. Always has. But she has blinders on. In her eyes, Dad never makes a mistake."

"And you walk without blinders?"

"No, I just walked away. I left Auburn five years ago."

"And built quite a successful career for yourself, your grandfather told me. What about your brother?"

"He still lives at home in the basement apartment. Rent free. Mom thinks he can do no wrong, either."

Worried that she was leaving the wrong impression with Jon, she said hastily, "Mom is sweet. Very generous with her time in local charities. And she's a marvelous cook. You'll discover that for yourself when you meet her tonight."

"She doesn't sound like your grandfather's daughter."

"They're an odd match. Totally different."

Jon drummed the tabletop with his fingers. "I'm sorry we're having dinner at your house this evening."

Embarrassed, she said, "Don't be. My parents are

gracious to their guests." *At least, I hope they will be.*

"That isn't the problem." The crinkle lines around his eyes deepened. "If we weren't otherwise engaged, I would have liked to take you out to dinner. Just the two of us, talking. Like we are now."

"I'd like that, too. Maybe some other time."

His fingers drummed on. "We'll have trouble getting around the university rules. You know there's no fraternizing between professors and students."

"That's for the undergraduate students, Jon."

He looked relieved. "Good. I'm only in town for a year. Not much time to get acquainted with you before I go back overseas."

"You're really going back?"

"You're going away at the end of the year, aren't you?"

"Yes, for my Ph.D. in biology."

He moved his hand across the table toward hers and touched her fingers. "Would you consider finishing your studies in Europe?"

She laughed, secretly thrilled at his interest. "We haven't even had dinner and you're already planning my future."

His banter matched hers. "Tobin, for the last hour, I have not been able to contemplate a future without you."

She felt a surge of blood rush along her neck. A tingle began in the pit of her stomach. She licked her lips and found them dry. Tried to clear her throat and found it too tight.

I will not blush, she thought. *I will not let this*

stranger tease me. And yet as she met his gaze, she could not be certain whether his words were an untrustworthy combination of flirtation and flattery or whether he indeed spoke the truth from his heart.

He glanced at the bill, reached for his money clip and laid out some bills. "Shall we go, Tobin?"

Outside, he said, "Let me give you a lift home."

"It's just a mile and it's a lovely day."

"That's why I want to spend more of it with you."

As they drove along, she asked, "What about your family, Jon?"

"As I mentioned, my parents are dead. Mom died twelve years ago, Dad two years later. There I was at twenty-four with no ties. That's when I took my first overseas assignment."

A ball of worry knotted inside. "I meant your wife and children, Jon."

His eyes strayed from the traffic, met hers, turned away abruptly. "No wife. I was engaged once. She was hit and killed by a car in London, a stone's throw from Westminster Abbey."

"Oh, Jon, I am sorry."

"No need to be. It's been eight years."

But you still feel the pain. She waited.

"I was in London to cover another IRA threat. Jenna flew over to join me."

"She was European?"

"No, a fellow American. A journalist. A good one, too. Jenna was special, beautiful." He reached out and touched Tobin's hand again. "In a way she reminds me of you. Sensitive. Caring. Ambitious. And yet you're different.''

The tingling began in the pit of her stomach again and tightened as he admitted, "Jenna was expecting a baby when she died. I lost my fiancée and my child at the same time."

She fixed her eyes ahead. "Make a left at the next corner."

His tone turned edgy. "You're shocked?"

"Numb. If Dad gets curious tonight, it's something you won't want to mention—the baby, I mean."

"Jenna and the baby are part of my past, Tobin. Part of me."

As he pulled to a stop in front of the parsonage, she said, "Dad wouldn't understand."

"Do you? Whatever happened to forgiveness, Tobin?"

"Sometimes Dad is a bit short on it."

He laughed sardonically. "And he's a pastor?"

"He stumbles over perfection," she said softly. "Like we all do." She stepped from the car before Jon had time to whip around to assist her. Standing there by the open door, she smiled up at him. "Thanks for the lift."

"My pleasure."

He said it as though he meant it, and she felt unfamiliar stirrings inside. Pleasure and embarrassment. Yearning. She was aware of his masculinity, the scent of his cologne, the amusement in his eyes. But there was a distance now. The warm, friendly man of an hour ago had slipped away. "I'd better go in, Jon."

"Wait. What about you, Tobin? Have you ever married?"

"No, not yet."

"You're waiting for the perfect one?"

"I've had other priorities. But I want God's choice for me when the time comes."

Stiffly he said, "And I wouldn't be God's choice?"

"Oh, Jon, I don't know. We just met."

"That was hours ago. Tobin, I believe in God."

"Believing isn't enough. It has to be more personal."

"That's how I see it. Between God and me. So no sermons."

"No sermons," she promised. "I'll see you this evening."

His frown was quickly replaced with awareness. "That's right. Dinner with the Michelsons. Then you will be there?"

I wouldn't miss it, she thought. "Gramps asked me to be there. I'm the family buffer."

He glanced beyond her, past the well-kept lawns to the two-story house with its white shutters and large porch. "It blows my mind to think I'm having dinner at a parsonage."

"Mother's a good cook."

"So your grandfather claims—but a parsonage. That will be a first for me. That large church that we passed—"

"That's the one. Dad's been there for twenty-five years."

"About time for a change, isn't it?"

She sighed. "Be prepared. Dad may ask you if you've settled on a church yet."

He looked surprised. "I told you, I'm not a religious man. I don't go to church. I get all the discipline I need at the boardinghouse where I'm staying."

"There's no comparison."

"Oh, yes. It's packed with strangers. Two coaches from the football team. A young kid called Wally, the nephew of the woman who owns the boarding home. Wally is quarterback on the football squad. The man in the room beneath mine is a banker. Haven't even met the sixth occupant. Our paths never cross."

"Do you like where you're living?"

He considered. "I'm used to living in a sleeping bag, catching a plane to another country on a moment's notice. And here I am in a house where the boarding lady insists that the beds be made every day and the wet towels dumped in the hamper."

"Good training," Tobin said.

"For what?"

She felt the crimson build at the base of her neck and rise to her cheeks. To cover her embarrassment, she said, "Being religious is not a prerequisite for coming to dinner tonight. Dad's quite political—intelligent. Well-read. You'll find him a good conversationalist. You will come?"

"As long as you're there. At seven then?"

"Come a little before. Gramps always does."

Chapter Three

The dining area in the Michelson home was a pleasant room with wide curtainless windows that allowed the sunshine to pour in during the daytime. Now with dusk already settling, the gardens and trees of the backyard were mere shadows as everyone took their seats around the long oak table.

"We won't wait for Kedrick," Tobin's father announced. "He was probably delayed at work."

Tobin glanced anxiously at her father. Ross Michelson sat stiffly, a stiffness that brought out his prominent cheekbones and that rigid set of his jaw. She saw herself in that distinctive Michelson image. His flaxen hair, lighter than her mother's, was rapidly turning silver and thinning on top.

"Smells good," Jon said as he eyed the sliced roast beef in front of him. "It's been mostly casseroles at my boardinghouse."

Wini Michelson's dark, sparkly eyes radiated

warmth and friendliness. "Then you must come back often."

Jon smiled across at Tobin. "I'd like that."

"Tobby, dear, make certain he comes again soon." She seemed distracted now, flustered as she glanced at the empty chair and unraveled her linen napkin. "But I think I burned the gravy."

"Either you did or didn't," Ross told her.

"I like my gravy brown like that," Gramps countered. "Dig in, Woodward. Let's show this cook how much we appreciate her."

Jon already had the meat platter in his hand when Tobin's father suggested they take time to give thanks.

"Already thanked my daughter," Gramps grumbled.

"I had Someone else in mind."

"Never mind, dear. Let's just eat. The food's getting cold."

Tobin breathed a sigh of relief as her father yielded. "All right, Wini," he said calmly. "I'll pray silently."

But he did so with his eyes open and his scowl settling on his wife and daughter. Tobin wondered what had gone wrong before the meal. Something at church? Something in the kitchen while her mother made gravy? Something between her father and Kedrick? Or the usual argument as to where the guests would sit?

Her mother liked to keep Gramps and Tobin's dad separated at the table. But not this evening. Gramps and Jon sat on either side of her father, looking like warriors about to do battle—and not even knowing when the battle would strike.

Jon is right, she thought. Twenty-five years is too long in the same church. Maybe too long in the same town. It's time for a change. Or was the change needed inside her father? Is that why she felt compelled to come home for the year to help the family find its way back to the happiness that had once existed? Her father had been happy once, but since coming home she had noticed the deep worry lines around his mouth, the shadows around his eyes. Always a mild-mannered man, he seemed distant from the peace he preached about on Sunday mornings.

Her gaze strayed to her brother sauntering into the room, a smirk tugging at his mouth. He slid innocently into the chair across the table from her and grabbed the vegetable dish.

"Ked, where have you been with my car all day?"

"Out and about, sis. I'll need it again in the morning."

She shook her head. "A definite no. I need it for school."

"But my van's still in the shop."

"Oh, Tobin, darling," Wini whined. "Can't you loan it to your brother? Gramps keeps him so busy at the newspaper."

Gramps went on chewing, but said, "So busy, Wini, that he doesn't even use the time card."

Cornered, Tobin's mother did what she always did to avoid a confrontation. She turned away and flashed a generous smile at her guest. "Mr. Woodward, Dad tells me you're a photojournalist."

A bite of roast dangled on Jon's fork. "Yes, but this year I'm teaching at the university."

"My daughter is studying there again."

"Yes. I suggested that she study abroad next year."

"That's a foolish idea," Ross said. Her father's cheeks blotched as her own were doing.

"Not when you enjoy her company as I do, Mr. Michelson."

Watching Jon, Tobin felt her fingers tingle again. She liked the way he faced off with her father with an easygoing grin.

"I've asked your daughter to be a model in one of my courses," he challenged.

"Not if I have anything to say about it." The silverware rattled as her father's fist hit the table.

"Ross, dear, please. Mr. Woodward is a guest in our home."

"And his suggestion is preposterous, Wini. We have a reputation to live up to in this town."

Jon hid his surprise. "So do I, sir. I don't intend to betray my reputation as a photojournalist."

"And I don't intend for my daughter to be your model."

"Come on, Dad," Kedrick said sourly. "He doesn't plan to put my sister up in front of the classroom in nothing but a sheet. Woodward is not an artist. He's a photographer."

"And, Dad, I make my own decisions," Tobin said hotly.

Jon kept his cool. "For the sake of peace, Tobin, I withdraw my invitation."

"Ross, get off your high horse," Gramps said. "Jon here has photographed every major event in Europe in the last ten years."

"Not every one, Mr. Reynolds, but a good number of them."

"Kindly remember my daughter is not a major event."

In spite of his retort, Ross seemed more accepting of his guest by the time dessert arrived. A few minutes later, Gramps was dozing in his chair, her father more pleasant, her mother chatting incessantly. Kedrick stirred his third cup of black coffee—his hand shaking as he lifted the cup to his lips. Tobin thought they were home free for the rest of the evening when Ross abruptly turned the conversation back to Auburn.

"Are you a man of the church, Mr. Woodward?"

The unexpected question brought Gramps to with a start. Jon's hazel eyes lost their luster. "If you're asking me if I attend, sir, then the answer is rarely. It hasn't been one of my priorities. If you're asking if I believe in God, of course."

"You should join us on Sunday."

"No need, sir. I have my own type sanctuary."

K. T. Reynolds's bushy brows arced together. "Careful, Jon. You don't want to rile my son-in-law here. But I understand you. I haven't done much sitting on a church pew myself. Don't even know for certain there's a God."

"Oh, I know there's a God, K.T.! We even have chats now and then—mostly when I'm dodging bullets trying to get a photo, or when I'm picking up some half-starved kid and wondering where God was when the kid came down with AIDS.''

Tobin's stomach knotted as a deathly stillness hovered over the room. She tried to catch her father's eye to warn him off. He pursued relentlessly, marking the table linens with his fork tine before saying, ''You seem to take no caution regarding your own health, young man.''

''A kid dying of AIDS and starvation needs a friend, not a mask and sterile gloves.''

''A friend?'' Kedrick mocked. ''Is that what photojournalism is all about? Gramps has me covering major sporting events. Why don't you try me with something international, Gramps?''

''Prove yourself trustworthy and I will.''

Jon intervened. ''Why don't we talk sometime, Kedrick? We could take our cameras and go off to the mountains on Sunday.''

Kedrick leaned forward. ''You're serious?''

''Yes, we might even get Tobin to go along with us.''

''My children have been brought up in the church, Mr. Woodward. I prefer that they don't go hiking on Sunday.''

''Sir, I think we'd better let them decide.''

A wall had shot up between Jon and her father again. Tobin cleared her throat. ''More coffee, Mr. Woodward?''

Polite moments later, Jon stood and thanked his host. ''The meal was wonderful, but I really must be going, Mrs. Michelson.''

Tobin saw him to the door. "I'm sorry about what happened."

"Is that how your father treats every guest?"

"No, he's usually quite gracious to strangers.... But he thinks we're friends. He saw you bring me home earlier today."

"And that's a no-no. Good grief, Tobin, you're almost twenty-seven years old. You should pick your own friends."

"I know," she said softly. "But you have two strikes against you. You're my grandfather's friend and you seem to be kindred spirits when it comes to the church."

"I'm serious about the mountains on Sunday. What about it?"

"I can't, Jon. Some other time. Some other day."

He paused, then finally said, "Sure, some other time, then." He was on the porch, his face shadowed in the darkness, but she was certain that his brilliant eyes were no longer smiling.

Jon's voice turned even frostier. "Good night, Tobin."

She felt annoyed. She didn't want him walking off this way—going away thinking that she was immature, unable to choose her own friends. Things had felt so promising this afternoon over coffee, but now it all seemed ruined somehow. She liked the way he stood up to her father. Liked the sensitivity that he showed when he spoke of the child with AIDS. Jon was different. Someone that she wanted to know better. She still wanted to apologize for her family, to tell him that she was sorry for her mother's reticence, her brother's rudeness, her father's arrogance.

Good night. He might as well have said goodbye. But you're not slipping through my fingers that easily, she thought. If one of us says goodbye, I'll be the one.

Behind her, her grandfather made his own way to the door. He leaned down and kissed her cheek. "Make any plans with Mr. Woodward?" he asked conspiratorially.

"What plans?"

"With Mr. Woodward."

"He went through the door and that was it." She slipped her arm in his to detain him. "Gramps, why did you want him to come to dinner? You knew it wouldn't turn out well."

"I wanted you two to get together. You've been gone five years and you still came home single. I'm just helping you out."

"Well, Jon wasn't impressed. The only way to force myself on him is to sign up for one of his classes. What do you think?"

"Bit late for that." He screwed up the tip of his nose. "How long has school been in session? Two weeks? Three?"

"You could pull strings. I could sign on as an audit."

"You're taking a full load in biology."

"But if I audit Jon's class, it won't be any work."

He shook his head. "You're going about this all wrong. You'd just be one more student in a sea of faces. He'd never take notice of you that way."

"Then what do you suggest, Gramps?"

He chuckled. "Do what I did with your grandmother. I ran a headline that said I loved her. Whole town knew."

"I thought you only printed news."

"It was news to Katelyn. She didn't know I existed when the newspaper went to print. She stormed into my office, raging mad."

Tobin took the bait and asked what she had asked more than once over the years, "So what happened, Gramps?"

Sudden tears glistened in her grandfather's eyes. "I proposed to her again that day. And when she turned me down I ran another headline. Katelyn Meyers Considers Proposal Of City Editor. Sold more papers that day than I had for a long time."

"That won't work for me. It would just announce to every girl on campus that Jon Woodward is single."

"Not every girl on campus will care." He sighed. "I'm telling you, it worked with Katelyn. How I miss that woman."

"So do I, Gramps." Lightly, she said, "Come on, what do you say? You could call the university president and pull strings and get me into Jon's class."

He freed himself from her clutch and finger-combed his snow-white hair. As he stepped out on the porch, he turned back, the porch light reflecting on his pudgy face. "We'll bargain, dear. You come on staff part-time at the *Herald*—"

"I can't spare the hours."

"Then you don't have time to audit Woodward's class."

"I can't think of any other way. I just have to apologize to him. Otherwise, he won't come back, not after the way Dad preached at him."

"I come back. And Ross has been preaching at me for thirty years. No reason to miss Wini's good cooking," he reasoned.

"Gramps, just today Jon asked me what's wrong with forgiveness. I have to let Jon know that God is bigger than the limits Dad puts on Him."

"Put that way, sweetheart, you almost have me believing in a Higher Power."

"You will some day."

"Maybe," he grunted.

She hugged him. "But don't wait too long. I love you too much for that."

Gramps walked to his car without looking back and became a shadow beneath the maple tree. Tobin heard his car door open and shut, the sputter of his engine as he took off in jerking spurts.

She locked the door and went slowly up the stairs, one tired foot after the other. Allowing the moon to light a path for her across the darkened bedroom, she stood by the windows gazing across campus toward the boardinghouse on Maple Street. Even if Gramps didn't help her, she'd think of something. Jon Woodward was the first man who had appealed to her in a long time. She paused with her hand on the windowpane. What was it that attracted her to him? Was it just an apology?

Chapter Four

On Monday morning Tobin raced from the Oceanographic Institute over to the communications building and barged into Jon Woodward's class ten minutes early. She paused in the doorway, noticing both the empty seat on the second row and the young woman with sun-blond hair sitting beside it.

Something in the girl's expression and those quick-witted, intelligent eyes looked familiar. Her memory stirred. Tobin had definitely seen the girl before. Her skin was exceedingly fair, her eyes a vivid blue, her high cheekbones flushed with natural beauty. *Jade Wellington!* No wonder she had recognized the name when Jon mentioned it.

"Jade." "Tobin," they exclaimed in unison.

"The shades of summer camp," Jade said. "Come and join me."

Tobin sank gratefully into the empty spot and caught her breath. Jade was still the same cute kid from camp and still putting style to whatever she wore. Her jeans fit smoothly over firm hips and a matching denim jacket lay on the floor beside her purse. But what really caught Tobin's attention was Jade's necklace, an emerald jewel with tiny diamonds surrounding it.

"Fancy finding you here in Auburn, Jade."

"My folks moved here after Dad retired."

Distracted, Tobin cried, "I was in such a hurry I forgot my camera."

Jade dismissed Tobin's worry with a wave of her hand. "I'll loan you one of mine. But if you're just joining this class, you must have pull somewhere. Woodward throws assignments at you and expects them in on time. You'll have to make up everything."

"So why are you taking the class?"

She said flippantly, "I did it with an eye to my future."

In the weeks ahead, Tobin would remember those words, but for now all she heard was Jade nonchalantly saying, "Woodward is a famous photographer. And he's good at what he does."

"So I hear. What do I do with this? It's my permission slip to audit the class. University seal and all."

Jade's pencil-thin brows arched as she glanced at the official paper in Tobin's hand. "Woodward won't like that. I know firsthand. He expects full participation. No bench sitters."

Tobin found herself snapping back, "Jade, I can't spare the time. I can just do the lectures."

"Woodward's big on the labs. Five of the students dropped out the first week, once they realized he expected them to work for a grade.'' She winked mischievously. ''We still have five minutes before he gets here. He usually cuts in just under the wire as the bell rings. I should know. He's an old friend of my brother's and they were always running late.''

She wiggled her shiny upturned nose, warding off a sneeze. ''Let's put that permission slip up on his desk. Maybe he won't notice it until after class, then you can barter with him. He's easy to look at—easy to talk to.''

She took the paper from Tobin and tapped the shoulder of the young man in front of her. ''Be a good sport, Wally, and stow this on Woodward's desk.''

He cocked his head and looked at her. Flexing his muscles, he said, ''If you cut my hair after the game on Saturday, Jade.''

''You make a touchdown for me, Wally, and you're on.''

He snatched the note from her fingers and sauntered to the front of the room, slapped the signature card faceup on the professor's desk and came back to his seat grinning. ''Welcome to slavery,'' he said, eyeing Tobin.

''Don't listen to Wally,'' Jade warned. ''You'll like Woodward if he allows you to audit his class. But don't be surprised—''

''I can only audit. I'm at the Oceanographic Institute.''

''Graduate school? I'm here on an undefined major. Someday I'll make up my mind what I want to be. So what are you doing in an undergrad course like this?''

Tobin looked down at her polished nails and then back to the curious eyes, unwavering as they met Tobin's gaze.

"I'm interested in photography," Tobin murmured.

Now the unblinking eyes teased. "And not the professor? Half the girls in the class have their eyes on him. You'll have to sign up.... I did. I couldn't even make first base with him at the house, so I signed up for his class." More seriously, she said, "I still remember the day I met you, Tobby."

Yesterday came winging back—twelve years ago as clear as a fast-running stream. The redwoods towered above them. The smell of pine needles and damp earth filled the air. The tiny log cabin had been cramped with eight campers and a counselor. Colorful sleeping bags stretched out on the hard, narrow bunks. The girls had giggled into the late hours of the night while the counselor dozed fitfully. Tobin couldn't even remember the counselor's name, but she remembered Running Springs Camp up in the Santa Cruz Mountains. And Jade Wellington—the kid in the upper bunk.

"I was supposed to be your big sister and help you through your first camp experience," Tobby said.

"And you hated the responsibility."

"I know. I kept thinking you were just a kid."

"I was. Three years younger than you. Remember, my folks left me off at camp the wrong week. Mom got the dates mixed up."

"Their dumping you off like that caused quite a ruckus."

"I didn't want them hanging around, so Daddy

shoved the registration fee into my hand and drove off with Mother.''

"The camp director couldn't reach them by phone to tell them to come back to pick you up."

"I'm not surprised. They went off to San Francisco on a holiday of their own. That's when the counselor assigned you to watch over me for the whole week. I was a real drag, wasn't I?"

Homesick as a kitten, Tobin remembered. "I heard you up in the upper bunk, wheezing, night after night. I figured you were crying. I decided you were nothing but a big baby."

"It was my asthma."

"You never said anything about asthma. I wish you had."

"Didn't figure it was anyone's business. I'd lived with it all my life. Daddy always called them my twitchy lungs. Said if Teddy Roosevelt could go on to be a president, I could be anything I wanted to be, too."

"Teddy Roosevelt had asthma?"

"Lot of famous people do."

"We figured it was just an excuse when you went into a fit of coughing every time it was your turn to sweep the cabin."

"Couldn't help it. Spring pollens and dust always set me off. In seconds my chest would be tight as a drum. Inside I was no different than other kids. It's just my lungs didn't know it. I wanted to prove myself to you guys. I wanted you to like me."

"Well, you won me over that last morning when we had the swimming contest. While I was testing the water with my toes, you plunged in and swam. You put us all to shame. Do you still swim?''

''As often as I can.''

''You do know about the swim team here at the university?''

''I'm on it.''

''Your asthma won't hold you back?''

''It never did. Besides, I outgrew it as I got older. Barely ever have trouble with it now. Tobin, I'm glad I was good at something back at camp. Your friends didn't want me around.''

''I felt guilty about that for weeks afterward. And I didn't know where you lived or how to phone you.''

''You never asked me about myself at camp.''

''I was a pretty rotten big sister.''

Jade nodded. ''But under the circumstances, I didn't blame you. You weren't used to having a young kid tag along after you.''

''The truth is, you really made me mad that night when you crawled down from the upper bunk and put your foot in my face. I thought you were an intruder.''

Jade was thoughtful. ''I kept trying to hush you up. You were a preacher's kid or something.''

Tobin chewed at her lower lip. ''Still am.''

''You had a good-looking twin brother.''

''Still do, and he's better looking than ever. But tell me—what in the world were you doing that night climbing down from the upper bunk at two in the morning? It was pitch-dark when you left the cabin. You were coughing, weren't you?''

''Yeah, my asthma was getting to me. That's when I dumped my duffel bag inside out looking for my bronchial dilator. And all you did was yell at me, so I left the cabin to get away from you.''

''And then I had to lie there worrying about you prowling around in the dark.''

''I wanted to be alone.'' Jade touched the emerald necklace, wrapping one finger around the chain. ''I was checking God out.''

''And that's the night you found Him. I remember you telling us about it at the fireside the night before camp broke up.''

A long silence passed between them as other students made their way into the classroom, chatting amiably as they slammed their books onto their desktops and slouched into the seats.

''I'd almost forgotten that, Tobin, but I did find Him. I even promised God I'd walk with Him the rest of my life.''

Her wide blue eyes lost their luster. For a moment she seemed fragile-winged, balancing on a leaf, ready to take flight.

''Did you keep that promise?'' Tobin asked gently.

''I'd almost forgotten I made it.'' Despair shadowed her face. ''When camp split up, I kept hoping you'd want to be my friend. You know, the little kid looking up to the high school freshman. You didn't even come to see me off when my parents picked me up.''

''I did give you a rough time, didn't I? I'm sorry, Jade.''

''No big deal. I survived.''

The warmth of Jade's forgiving smile touched Tobin. ''Jade, is it too late to be friends now? I'm just back in town after being gone five years. So why don't we get together this weekend?'' she suggested.

"I'd like that, Tobby."

Woodward barreled into the room, his arms laden with books, a heavy camera bag on one shoulder. He lined the books up on his desk and slipped his arm free from the camera bag. A frown lined his brow as he unpacked the satchel.

He's seen my petition to audit, Tobin thought.

With slow deliberate motions, Jon rested his hands against the chair back and glanced around the room, his eyes settling briefly on Tobin. She knew in that glance that he was not happy with her. He whirled around to the blackboard and chalked in the assignments. When he faced the class again, he was in control.

Tobin tried to concentrate on his lecture, but found herself listening to his well-modulated voice. She tried to focus on the cameras that he held in his hands from time to time, but found herself unable to take her eyes from his face.

Woodward didn't look Tobin's way again until the fifty-minute lecture ended. Then he picked up her permission slip and said, "Miss Michelson, may I see you immediately after class?"

"I warned you," Jade whispered as she gathered up her books and tossed her denim jacket over one shoulder. "There's fire in Woodward's eyes. Now you're really in for a lecture."

Tobin squirmed. It wasn't the fire she wanted to see. "Why don't you just stay with me, Jade? Ease me out of this one."

"No, I'm out of here." She balanced her books and jacket and fished for a business card. "Just in case you don't make it back into class, that's my number. Call me."

Tobin glanced down at the card as Jade left the room. J. Wellington, Hair Stylist, the card said. And in the middle: Jade's Cuts and Styling. By appointment only.

So that's the path she took? Tobin thought. She's a beauty operator. A plucky, enterprising hairstylist without a shop, but not without customers. Jade was using her skills to work her way through college. But she had to be all of twenty-three. Why had it taken so long to come back to the halls of ivy? Had Jade been serious when she said that her major was undefined—that she was still trying to decide what she wanted to do with her life?

The room was totally empty now, the last of the students dragging through the door into the wide corridor.

"Well, Miss Michelson?" Professor Woodward said.

She looked up. He was stacking his books methodically and packing his camera bag, but his eyes were on her. "You're unhappy with me in your class," she said meekly.

He paused. "Shouldn't I be?"

"Gramps pulled strings to get me in. He told the president that I use photography in my work as a marine biologist."

"So that's how you made it? Didn't K.T. stretch the truth?"

"No, I use photography all the time. I had to take your class. I couldn't think of any other way to apologize to you."

He zipped the camera bag. "You don't owe me an apology."

"But I was embarrassed over the way my father treated you."

"Then let your father apologize."

"Oh, Jon—Professor Woodward, I mean—Dad doesn't even know he was rude. He hasn't always been like that."

"Like I told you, Tobin, he should find a new parish."

She turned crimson. "Dad's under great stress these days."

"Because of your brother?"

"I don't know. Problems at the church, maybe."

"Then my attending wouldn't help matters."

He walked over to the classroom door and shut it and then came back and slipped into the seat that Jade had occupied. "It looks like you and Miss Wellington are friends." There was a question in his words—or was it concern in his voice?

"We met years ago at summer camp. I'm going to enjoy getting better acquainted with her."

"She could do with a good friend. She's a good student," he said absently. "Now, if she could just settle on a major. You could encourage her with that. You're so goal oriented."

"Isn't Miss Wellington?"

"She could be with the right influence. She's had a rough time for a few years, but things are looking better for her. I think she'd make an excellent photographer.''

He was being professional, not even mentioning that he knew Jade and her family outside the classroom. Why was he guarding their friendship? Tobin felt a sudden tinge of envy. "Do you know as much about each of your students?" she challenged.

"A few. Now, what about us?" he asked abruptly.

"Us?"

"Tobby, I can't let you audit my class, not when the fraternizing rule applies to undergraduates.''

"I'm not an undergraduate, Jon.''

"But this class is. And the president at this university is a tough old boy. A stickler with rules.''

"I thought rules were made to be broken.''

He faced her, his eyes amused. "Not according to your dad. You'll have to drop my class just to keep peace in your family.''

"Then I might not see you again.''

He ran his knuckle down her cheek. "We'll find a way. I want to spend every spare moment with you.''

"I don't have any spare moments. I'm taking a full course.'' She glanced at the clock above the chalkboard. "And if I don't hurry, I'm going to be late getting back to the institute.''

"So taking my class is time-consuming?" He smiled, his thoughts unhurried. "I'll think of something. But the rule about dating students still stands. I want to be free to take you out.''

"It didn't sound that way the other night, Jon.''

"I've had time to think about that. I won't let your

father come between us. Maybe we can go mountain hiking after church?''

"You'll go to church, then?''

"No. But we could go out Sunday afternoon?''

"Does your invitation include Kedrick?''

"Not this time.''

Jon stood and held out his hand. Her own felt small and cold in his as he pulled her up beside him. She sensed his closeness—fought the tingling that rose inside her.

"Drop my course and leave it to me. I'll talk to the university president this afternoon and offer my photographic skills for the Oceanographic Institute. I'll tell him we're planning a project together.''

"The two of us? That wouldn't be the truth.''

He smiled patiently. "It will be. You spend your Saturdays on an oceanographic vessel, don't you?''

"Twice a month.''

"I'll offer to do a photo shoot for them on those same Saturdays. Your father can't oppose that, can he?''

"Not if he doesn't know about it.''

He leaned down and brushed a kiss across her lips. "Where do you study at nights?''

"The research library at the institute.''

"Not at home?''

"Not very often.''

"Good. I'll see you there this evening. And afterward,'' he said smiling, "we'll grab something to eat and then I'll give you a ride home.''

"But I have my car.''

His eyes twinkled. "Let Kedrick borrow it.''

"I'll ask him at dinner. He can drop me off at the library. Jon—do you like molasses cookies?"

"I love cookies. Any kind."

"We can have some when you take me home this evening."

"But your father—"

"He retires early. Once he's asleep, he won't hear a thing."

"Sounds good to me." He leaned down and this time his kiss was lingering, more persuasive.

Chapter Five

Three weeks later Tobin tumbled out of bed early on Saturday morning and was showered and dressed and downstairs for breakfast before she realized she was not alone. She caught the aroma of bacon as she reached the foot of the stairs and smiled to herself. Mom up early? she wondered. Or Kedrick? No, Kedrick slept in late on Saturdays and her mother always reserved bacon and waffles for Sunday morning.

She burst into the kitchen and was even more startled to find her father standing by the stove, scrambling eggs. "Dad, what are you doing up so early?"

He turned her way, his eyes troubled, his fair hair more silver than she had ever noticed before. "Couldn't sleep."

"You're not ill?"

"No, I wanted to have breakfast with you."

The table was already set, the orange juice poured. She gave him a quick hug, her eyes on the kitchen clock. "I think I can spare fifteen or twenty minutes, but I'm due at Birchport Harbor by seven-thirty. It's my Saturday with the institute."

"Out to sea on board one of their oceangoing vessels, eh?" He took in her attire with a scowl, expressing his displeasure at her cutaway shorts and an old sweatshirt of Kedrick's when he asked, "Dressed like that?"

She glanced down. At least her crew socks and stark white canvas shoes were new. "We go casual. We have to handle enormous nets and rope coils and all sorts of specimens."

"You're not diving again this morning?"

"Don't worry about me, Dad. It's all part of my job."

He popped the muffins in the toaster and divided the eggs and bacon. "Pour some coffee for us, honey."

When he dropped into the chair across from her, she saw the weariness in his eyes as he said, "I haven't seen much of you these last few weeks, Tobby. I miss our old chats."

"I've been busy with my studies."

He nodded. "I know. But Kedrick tells us that you've been spending most of your time with Mr. Woodward."

"Some," she said, embarrassed.

"Mother and I hoped you'd spend more time with Kedrick."

"We've managed a game or two of tennis."

Dark circles crouched beneath his eyes, his brow rutted into frowns. Somewhere along the way he had dumped five or maybe even ten pounds, she noticed.

"Are you and Kedrick going golfing this morning, Dad?"

His jaw tightened. "You've been so busy, honey, you haven't noticed. Kedrick and I rarely speak these days."

"Is he really drinking that much?"

"I never ask, but I hear him coming in at three and four in the morning. I was hoping you'd be able to talk to him, Tobby. He'd listen to you." Sadly he said, "He's still your mother's pride and joy. She won't even discuss what's happening."

His shirt lay open at the neck, his chin sagging behind the collar. He was only fifty-eight, but he looked ten years older. Usually he wore a suit and tie or the clerical garb on Sunday. It was funny seeing him dressed this way—in a short-sleeve sports shirt and faded jeans, his wife's apron tied around his waist.

"Then call one of the elders and go golfing with him. You don't need Kedrick."

"But he needs us. Besides, I dropped my membership at the golf club."

"You didn't drop out because of Kedrick?"

Again his smile fell short. "It's hard to find a golf partner these days, sweetheart." He ran his hand through his thinning hair, recapturing for a second a touch of boyishness. "But honey, it's more than that. The deacon board suggested that I get my house in order if I can't fulfill the requirements of a shepherd."

"That's not fair, Dad. Look at their families."

"Mine is the one that matters. I'm the church leader. A bishop rules his house well, Tobin. Has control of his family." His voice cracked. "One of the men suggested that I resign."

"Not because of Kedrick?"

"They tell me my sermons no longer please them. They attack me. I attack the youth, trying to put a damper on some of their social events and liberal views. In spite of the university, Auburn is a small town. We can't hide in Auburn."

"You haven't done anything wrong, Dad."

"Lately, I haven't done anything right."

She leaned across the table. "Talk to Gramps."

He shook his head and ran his thumb around the brim of his coffee cup. "K.T. and I have never been on the same wavelength. He always wanted Kedrick to take over the newspaper when he retired. Now he tells me Kedrick isn't fit to do anything."

She longed to comfort him. What had happened to the smiling father of her childhood? Back then, he would scoop her into his arms and she would pat his cheeks and say, "Daddy, I love you."

Tobin couldn't even croak out the words right now. She still felt resentful that he had urged her to put a hold on her own career and come home for the year. Attending the institute was a good move, but except for Jon, it would have been better if she had stayed away from Auburn. She didn't want to watch Kedrick destroy himself with alcohol—and take the family down with him.

Glancing at her watch, Tobin knew she still had several minutes before she had to fly, before she would have an excuse to escape the parsonage.

"Maybe all of these things about Kedrick are nothing but rumors, Dad. I could call Brent Carlson."

"And ask him to turn his other cheek?"

"Well, he doesn't have to stop Kedrick every time he sees him on the highway."

"Honey, he's just doing his job. Brent is not the one who is drinking. I've talked to Brent. The next time they pick Kedrick up on a DUI, his license is gone." He refused to look at her. "Brent tried to get the judge to order Kedrick into a recovery program. Judge Nanry has avoided that so far—"

"Why is Carlson picking on our family?"

He gave her a dry chuckle as he poured a second cup of coffee. "Don't be hard on Brent, Tobin. He's a fine young man. A good police officer. This town could use more men like him."

"Dad, I was surprised to see him at church these last few Sundays. Is he there to spy on Kedrick?"

The tense facial muscles relaxed into a smile. "He's only been attending since you came back to town, Tobin. I don't think it's my sermons that lure him—I think it's my daughter. I've watched the way he looks at you, Tobby. He still likes you."

"It wouldn't work out. It didn't years ago. It won't now."

"Go gently with him, Tobin. Brent is more a friend to this family than we realize. Someday we may really need him—"

"That will be the day." She put down her cup, the bitter taste of coffee coating her tongue. "It seems like everything is piling in on you, Dad. Has my coming home made it worse?"

"Your coming home may be the only thing holding this family together. But there have been a few comments at church—about you dating one of the university professors."

"So they know about that? But, Dad, we've been discreet."

"That's what worries the elders. They say it's against the university rules for a professor to date a student."

"That rule applies to undergrads, Dad. Not to me. And I hardly call what we're doing going steady. I wish it were." She felt hot, boiling rage as she pushed the sleeves of her sweatshirt above her elbows. "Tell the deacon board that what I do outside the church is my business."

He finished his eggs. "You and Woodward—is it serious? I couldn't bear it if I had to worry about both you and Kedrick."

"I'm just going out with Jon. I'm not getting speeding tickets or being picked up for DUIs, Dad."

"At least Brent Carlson attends church, Tobby. He'd be a nice man for you."

She nibbled a strip of bacon. "Kedrick wouldn't thank me for dating a policeman. Not when they're at odds."

"Sweetheart, I'm not trying to make you unhappy about Jon Woodward. He's a good man. But you can't build a stable relationship with a man who finds no time for a living God."

"You don't know that for certain."

It took all his effort to say, "Sometimes I feel I

have failed you and Kedrick. I never meant to be a rotten father."

"Don't say that. You've been good to us."

"But Kedrick tells me it hasn't been enough. He says I've driven both of you from the church."

"Dad, I'm in church every Sunday."

"Bodily, yes. But I think your heart wanders. Why don't you bring Mr. Woodward this Sunday? And then have dinner with us afterward. Your mother would like that."

"You didn't exactly impress Jon the last time he was here. Jon is a private man where matters of the heart and faith are concerned. I can't question his communion with a Holy God."

"You must, Tobby, or I'm afraid that your own communion will shatter over the matters of the heart. Honey, I know you're a grown woman. A beautiful one. But I don't want you hurt. Woodward will be going back to Europe at the end of the school year."

"Maybe I'll go with him."

Her father pressed his tented fingers against his lips. "You told me once that you wouldn't marry anyone outside the church."

She laughed sardonically. "Who said anything about marriage? Aren't you rushing things a bit, Dad?"

Tobin thought of Jenna and Jon's unborn child. Thought of the feelings that Jon's presence stirred deep within her. She gathered up her plates and silverware and carried them to the sink. "Dad, I have to go. I'm already running late."

She slipped her arm around his shoulders and

kissed the top of his head. "I love you, Dad. You know that. Everything will work out. You'll see."

But would they work out? she wondered as she paused in the doorway. She had long ago made a commitment to God to stay pure, to wait until marriage for the intimacy of the marriage bed—that deep longing for oneness that stirred in the heart of every woman. In hers, as well. And here she was brushing aside her father's concern and bartering with God that Jon Woodward might be that one.

"Thanks for breakfast, Dad."

"Be good to those sea turtles today," he said lightly. "And don't take any risks on a dive."

"I won't. That's why I ate lightly. I'm always careful."

She took her research assignments with the institute seriously. Today she would collect specimens from beneath the ocean surface and log in the findings when she went back on board. "I'll rehearse my diving techniques all the way to the harbor. I promise."

But as Tobin drove the twenty-five-minute stretch to Birchport Harbor, her thoughts strayed from loggerhead turtles and sea urchins to the day's outing on board the institute's vessel. Always before she ran on high octane, confident in her ability as a researcher. Today she wanted to make no mistakes. Jon would be watching her and she wanted to do her best.

She tried to play out the diving techniques that she would use, but she could think clearly on only one thing. Jon Woodward. And she couldn't even think clearly about him. He had walked into her life—no, she had walked into his, walked into her grandfather's newspaper office and discovered Jon. From the start he had kindled inside her something that was fresh and vital and distant from the family problems. But did she dare think of falling in love?

The two of them were opposites, yet kindred spirits. They had exciting careers, but different goals. Different destinations. They could talk for hours and never run out of words or sit in silence and still feel comfortable. But her dad was right. They viewed God from a different telescopic lens.

Even on their hikes in the mountains they viewed things differently. Tobin enjoyed the alpine flowers, Jon marveled at the towering evergreens that shaded them.

He talked about the formation of mountains—she worried about the empty bottles and soda cans left behind by other hikers, which ruined the environment. On their second hike, they had paused by the site of an old avalanche where parts of the majestic hills had roared down the mountainside the previous winter. Standing there, she was certain Jon saw God as power. But it was a distant recognition, not a personal one. Did she dare go on seeing him—dare allow herself to keep falling so deeply in love with him?

But to let Jon go, to break off a friendship before it had time to develop into something lasting was more than she wanted to face. Always before, she kept her open palms extended, wanting God's best in her life. Now she wondered why she had come back to Auburn. Until then, she'd had it all. A family who loved her. Loyal friends. A satisfying career. And contentment and fellowship with a living God.

So why had she allowed Jon to become so important? There had been other men, even more attractive than Jon. Colleagues at the aquarium and forest station and at church. Ski partners on the slopes. Dinner dates. Memorable times. But never before had she felt this all-consuming response to another human being. Jon awakened everything inside her. Pleasure and delight. Laughter and expectation. Excitement when she saw him. And after last night—a mistrust in herself. Had she led Jon on? Was she missing God's best?

Surely, God, she whispered as she accelerated and felt the tires squeal beneath her, *surely You didn't bring Jon into my life just to tempt me—just to force me to give him up?*

Tears burned behind her eyelids, smarting there, stinging and blinding. She flicked her right-hand signal and sped dangerously close to another driver as she thought about leaving the institute library last night and going for a moonlit drive with Jon. Of coming home and walking arm in arm up the walkway to the parsonage.

"I don't want to say good-night," Jon had said. "Not yet, Tobby."

Suddenly he was holding her in his arms, kissing her. She knew no one had ever stirred her like this.

Give it time, she told herself. Go slowly.

But they didn't have that much time. They would go their separate ways in a year. So far most of their dating had been like a secret rendezvous—sitting across from Jon at the Oceanographic Library, night after night. She'd look up from her biology text, pen poised, and catch him smiling at her. Afterward, they would walk hand in hand back to the car through the dimly lit parking lot and snack in out-of-the way places.

"Best if the students don't see us together," he had told her. But was that the real reason? What was going on in Jon's life that he refused to date her openly?

Three Sundays in a row he waited for her in the field behind the church parking lot, so far out that he didn't even hear the hymns through the open window. They stopped at a gasoline station so she could change and then they had the rest of the day together—just the two of them hiking and picnicking at the top of a mountain trail. Up there and at the midnight snacks at the parsonage—munching homemade cookies and drinking cocoa—they talked about the future. His future. Her future. Never their future. The chance to dress up in her finery and have him pick her up at the parsonage door was never an option.

Who were they hiding from? She remembered the girl he had lost in London, the baby that Jenna had carried to her death. Jon had wanted to spend his life with Jenna, too, but marriage had not taken priority. Tobin could not be jealous of a dead girl, but she questioned Jon's motives. Where would spending their spare moments together lead? Jon would be back in Europe soon. She would be on the East Coast working on her Ph.D. in biology, an ocean away from him. Was his time with her a passing fancy? A casual friendship to fill his hours in Auburn?

Don't do that to me, Jon, she thought. I take you

more seriously than that. I make commitments and keep them.

She passed the sign to Birchport Harbor and spun right without signaling, squealing on two tires. She wouldn't even have Jon to herself this weekend. Jade was coming over, eager to go trailblazing with them.

Chapter Six

Jon Woodward sped along the coast highway with
his windows down, the marvelous ocean breeze
brushing his face. The water looked calm, inviting,
like a sheet of glass as the sun reflected on it. He took
the last bite of a doughnut, the crumbs dropping to
his lap as his thoughts turned to the expectation of
spending the morning with Tobin. But he would keep
it professional. He must not endanger her career or
risk a verbal rebuttal from the university on fraternizing with a student. Grad student or not, he couldn't
risk rumors. Besides, he still wasn't certain himself.

Was he rushing pell-mell into a relationship that he
hadn't planned on? In the past few weeks they had
talked about future plans, but he wasn't even certain
how far his commitment to Tobin could go. Like her?
Yes, it was more than that. He constantly found himself thinking about her, then drawing back. Tobin was
terrific, but she was a Michelson. Jon could handle
the grandfather, even identify with him. He liked the

gruff old man and the quick chats and cups of coffee in K.T.'s cubicle at the *City Herald*. He knew the old man was trying to line him up with Tobin. But her twin brother and father were headaches Jon didn't need.

A breezy gust whipped through the car. Jenna was yesterday. Tobin today. But wipe Jenna out of his mind and memory? He was hanging on to his past while trying to throw out a lifeline to his future. No, the truth was he was leery of falling in love again, of tempting fate to snatch Tobin out of his life as Jenna had been snatched away.

Even more, he feared that Tobin would turn him down. Turn him down for what? So far his invitation to her had been some vague mention of living abroad next year so they could get better acquainted. He'd get right up to the word *marriage* and back off like a scared rabbit. Yet this morning he couldn't even imagine life without her. Marriage was big time. Lasting. If he went for it, he was in it for keeps.

For weeks he had refused to put his finger on the other problem, but he acknowledged it now when no one was listening. He'd hit thirty-four on a liberal upbringing. He had never needed church, hadn't considered God as any more than existing. In some of those miserable places in the world, when he dodged bullets with a camera balanced on his shoulder, he wondered where God was. When Jenna died, he blamed it on God. The day he buried her, he vowed he'd make it through life without teaming up with God.

And then he'd run into Angelo, that little kid in

Bosnia, and he had to depend on God to get the kid to safety. It had been a short-term acquaintance, but viewing it now, he knew that God had answered that prayer for Angelo's safety.

Jon had escaped a lot of other dangerous places in the world without a prayer. Now here he was in this town of twenty thousand—add the campus population to that—and a preacher's daughter, a beautiful young woman with dimpled cheeks and honest blue eyes, had walked into his life. If he could get Tobin out of Auburn, he'd have a fighting chance to change her into an independent free thinker who wouldn't swallow her father's church doctrine on hearsay.

Who you fooling, Woodward? he asked himself. Tobin is into this God business. It's personal with her. Crossing that ocean to Europe won't change her mind.

The coast road wound around the cliffs, dipping down now toward Birchport Harbor. The ocean was like a blue-and-green tapestry, ripples of azure green, ripples of cobalt blue.

Jon turned right at the Birchport lot and parked his car beside Tobin's. He donned his sunglasses, hoisted his camera equipment from the trunk and made his way along the dock to the institute's fleet of research vessels that lay anchored along the wharf. The *SeaBreeze,* the smallest of the craft, was little more than a ninety-foot yacht. The *SeaWind,* slightly bigger, had a refurbished exterior. Beside that lay the *SeaFern* with its European elegance. He stopped by the gangplank of the *SeaGull,* the one he would board, and shifted the weight of his camera bag as he took in the larger 188-foot *SeaFarer,* a luxurious, oceangoing vessel. An American flag and the Venetian red flag of the institute flapped at the mast.

As he boarded the *SeaGull,* he saw Tobin on the opposite side of the ship beside the water tanks and enormous coiled nets. She stood by a rope winch, her hand on the pulley, her face toward the ocean. Usually he thought of her as vulnerable, needing his protection, but he was seeing her in her world, confident and completely at ease.

"Professor Woodward," the captain said. "We'll be getting underway shortly. But let me give you a quick tour of the ship first."

Before following the captain he took another glance toward Tobin. She looked sturdy and efficient, and casual in cutaway shorts that revealed her attractive legs. She had pushed the sleeves of an old sweatshirt above her elbows, leaving her suntanned forearms bare. The sun cast shimmering glints of gold through her hair. He sensed the ship swaying beneath his feet, but felt more unbalanced by the pounding of his heart. He would catch some candid shots of Tobin later—and not for the institute.

Teak handrails led into the internal stairway and down to the U-shaped galley. The skipper pointed to the coffee urn. "We keep java brewing. Help yourself. We'll have lunch at sea or possibly while we're anchored off Newman Island."

Newman Island lay off the coast, visible from shore on clear mornings. He hadn't counted on two hours on the open waters. "I thought we were riding the coast to study the sea lions."

"Our plans changed. We've had some complaints about problems in Newman cove, so the institute's checking that out."

As they passed young men working on the deck, the skipper pointed out the fantail and layout of the *SeaGull*. He indicated the danger spots for Jon to avoid if they hit unusual weather, particularly the wet, slippery area around the holding tanks. The main salon and the staterooms gleamed with polished brass and light sycamore paneling. Murals of sea turtles and whales and migratory birds hung on the glossy walls.

"So get your sea legs on, Professor," the skipper told him.

Jon already regretted the two doughnuts on an empty stomach, but he tried to focus on the trip. This is a working voyage, he reminded himself. One I volunteered for—and not a pleasure trip.

"Woodward, this vessel has long-range capacity. We're equipped to reach any environmental disaster."

"Well, I hope we don't meet with any."

The skipper laughed and with pride in his voice said, "Don't worry, Professor, I have a crew of ten on board prepared to handle any emergency."

Jon followed the skipper into a pilot house filled with nautical charts and electronic gear. The captain put his hand to the wheel and looked every inch a man comfortable with his surroundings. "If you have any questions, Professor Woodward, my staff can help you."

Jon dropped his canvas bag on one corner of the chart table and took out two cameras. "Well, I'd better get busy."

They were barely offshore when Jon felt the ship dip with the first of the swells. What had looked like a calm sea from his car was more threatening as they moved into the open waters. Two hours later when they anchored off Newman Island near a deep blue lagoon, Jon was sweating, nauseated.

But he inserted another roll of film and focused on Tobin as she adjusted her goggles. She had replaced her sweatshirt with an orange wet suit and a buoyancy yellow vest that would inflate and deflate at various depths beneath the surface.

"Miss Michelson, you're not going over the side?" he asked. It was the first words he had said to her the whole trip.

She scowled back, and picked up her flippers. "That's what we do on our Saturday cruises."

"Wait. Turn your face to the sun, Miss Michelson. There. That's the right angle. Wait…give me one more shot."

The smile froze on her face as he snapped another series of pictures. Then Tobin stepped down the ladder into the water carrying a specimen bag and slurp gun with her.

"The gun, Captain," Jon asked. "What's that for?"

"It's used to suck in fish and specimens."

Jon snapped another picture as Tobin's head slipped beneath the surface. What if she didn't come back up and he hadn't even told her he loved her? *Loved her?*

What's wrong with you, Jon Woodward? he asked

himself. You let her go right into that water. "Captain, what's so important about this lagoon?"

"The institute says it's becoming a salty lagoon."

"That would kill marine life," Jon observed.

"An oil tanker spilled oil out here near Newman months ago. It takes almost a year to get back to normal, and now this added problem. The salt depletes oxygen and leads to rampant algae."

"Will it affect Miss Michelson and the other divers?"

"They have oxygen tanks."

As another ten minutes ticked away Jon asked, "What about jellyfish floating among the seaweed, or worse, sharks?"

"No sharks in this lagoon and, rest assured, our divers keep their eyes open for jellyfish." He seemed amused. "If you're concerned about Miss Michelson, she's an experienced diver."

He pointed to the clipboard by the railing. "When they come back up, they'll label their mud samples and put the specimens of fish and turtles and algae in the holding tanks. They'll check for pollution and oxygen levels back at the institute." The skipper gripped Jon's arm. "Hey, Professor, are you all right? You're seasick is my guess. Here, let's get you over to a bench."

Jon felt sweaty and nauseous and could only guess that the doughnuts were turning him green around the gills. He was still hanging over the rail when Tobin broke the surface thirty minutes after diving beneath the water. She handed her flippers and slurp gun up to the skipper and with a specimen bag slung over one shoulder climbed aboard. With great effort Jon focused his wide-angle lens as she appeared on deck, her hair wet and stringy, her skin glistening with sea drops.

"Angle your face this way, Miss Michelson," Jon called. "There, that's it."

He clicked the camera and then leaned over the rail again.

Seagulls wheeled overhead, squealing and screaming, diving for food. Tobin wanted to run to Jon, but she took the clipboard that the skipper handed to her.

"You'd better record what you saw down there, Michelson."

"But Professor Woodward?"

"A case of seasickness. He won't thank you for interfering, and that pretty blonde that I often see him with isn't on board."

"The blonde?"

"A pretty young woman on campus, but he's running a risk being seen with a student."

A blonde? She was clearly—even with wet, stringy hair—not a blonde. Now she felt as sick as Jon looked. "It's all right if she's a grad student."

"She's an undergraduate," the skipper said. "Here, Michelson, label your specimens and put them in the tank."

She wanted to put the blonde—whoever she was—in the holding tank, too, but she obeyed.

"Are you all right?" he asked.

"Fine. I'd better go below and change."

"With another two hours back to shore, the professor will be in no condition to walk, let alone drive back to Auburn.''

"His problem," Tobin said.

"No, our problem. You have your car with you, don't you, Michelson? Why don't you drive him back to his boardinghouse and I'll make certain his car gets there?"

She brushed the salty tears from her face. How could she face Jon? He must think her an utter fool. One thing was certain. He wasn't willing to listen to her father's sermon, and no wonder. Somewhere on campus there was a pretty blonde who had Jon's attention, perhaps his heart.

Okay, God, I'm getting the picture at last. Loving Jon should not have taken priority. Helping him now was something she could do. Avoiding the skipper's gaze, she said, "Yes, yes. I can drive the professor to Auburn. I'll do that for you." For him.

They drove back to Jon's boardinghouse mostly in silence, with Jon's head resting against the back of the car seat. He looked whipped, his sun-bronzed skin a chalky yellow.

But she was angry with him as she said, "Jon Woodward, what's wrong with you? I'm good enough to drive you back to your boardinghouse, but all morning long you acted as though you had never laid eyes on me."

"What do you mean? I couldn't take my eyes off you."

"Oh, yes, for photographs. Me going over the side

of the vessel. Me boarding again with my hair stringy wet.''

''Someone else must have taken that shot,'' he murmured.

''No, you took it. 'Look this way, Miss Michelson,''' she mimicked. '''Turn your face a bit more to the left, Miss Michelson. No, don't move—I want just the right angle, Miss Michelson.' Miss Michelson. I have a name, Jon Woodward.''

''I was using it.''

''Then why did you treat me like a stranger?''

He twisted in the seat beside her. ''We were on duty, Tobby. At a university function. I didn't want to put you in a compromising position. You have a reputation—''

''So do you. The captain told me you're stringing some blonde along.'' She flicked her damp hair back and steered with one hand. ''And I have brown hair, in case you haven't noticed.''

''I've definitely noticed. Pretty brown with gold streaks. Please, don't weave the car like that, Tobby. I'll be sick again.''

''Not in my car you won't.''

''Then pull to the side of the road.''

''I'll park when we get to your place. So who's the blonde?'' she whispered.

His voice grew harsh, impatient. ''Ask the skipper of the *SeaGull*. He seems to know all about it.''

''I didn't dare. I was afraid it was true. Is that why you only see me at the library or on hikes alone in the mountains? So no one will see us together?''

He brightened. ''You're jealous.''

She didn't flinch, but answered him honestly. "Of course I'm jealous. And you've given me reason to be."

"You know I don't like crowds."

"That's a laugh, Jon. The worldwide photojournalist doesn't like crowds. Judging from your photos, you spend precious little time away from them."

"It's my job and I'm good at it."

"Oh, stop it, Jon. Today just wasn't what I expected. With you there I kept making silly mistakes. I don't usually do that. I'm good at my job, too."

He rubbed his stomach. "It turned out to be a lousy day for me, too. I've never been seasick before."

"I thought you'd make a better sailor."

"I thought we'd stay closer to shore—not cross half the ocean to get to Newman Island. I didn't expect so many people to be on board, either. I wanted to be alone with you, Tobby."

She pretended it didn't matter, but her words gave her away. "You didn't want the blonde to see us together."

"Believe me, you and the skipper are the only two who seem to know about this blonde. Introduce her to me when you find her." He groaned. "So what do you really want from me, Tobby?"

"Do you want the truth?"

She caught his nod from a side glance and swallowed the lump in her throat. "I want you to take me in your arms."

"You certainly chose a lousy time for that. You're driving us in the thick of city traffic. So what's your second choice?"

Her throat felt tighter than a banjo string. "I want you to take me out on a real date."

"Isn't that what we've been doing for the last few weeks?"

"You know what I mean. I want the whole world to see us together. And I want you to come to the parsonage in your best suit and tie with a bouquet of flowers in your hand."

"Flowers for your father?"

"Flowers for me—preferably red roses."

"I don't even own a suit. Just tweed jackets and slacks."

"That's good enough for a candlelit dinner over in Birchport or a dinner cruise on the harbor."

"I'd never make it. Right now, I don't think I could look at water ever again—at least until tomorrow."

"You think I'm crazy."

"No, Tobby, just old-fashioned."

"I like the traditional ways."

"I don't fit that category, Tobby. I can't change. I'm who I am. I thought you knew how much I care about you."

"Did you expect me to play a guessing game?"

"I don't know what I expected. I just wanted to be with you. But this old-fashioned courting—"

"Dad courted mother that way. He still opens the door for her and takes breakfast up to her now and then. He probably did this morning. He was up early enough, having breakfast with me."

"Don't mention food," he said. "Have a little pity on me?"

She swerved. "What did you have for breakfast?"

"I was too early for breakfast at the boardinghouse so I grabbed coffee and doughnuts on the way to Birchport."

"Sugar. Pure sugar on an empty stomach. No wonder you were sick." She reached out and touched his hand. "You need someone to take care of you, Jon Woodward."

He lifted her hand to his lips, his lips moist against her smooth skin. "Do you have someone in mind?" he asked.

"What about the blonde or me? You make the choice."

He pressed his lips to her hand again. "I already have."

They fell silent as she maneuvered her car into a parking place in front of his boardinghouse.

"Come on," she said taking his arm as he stepped from the car, "I'm going to see you up to your room and make you a spot of mint tea."

"I just have a hot plate in the room and no tea bags."

"I carry a supply of tea for just such occasions."

She wondered as he climbed the steps with great effort whether he was playing his weakness for all it was worth. But he still looked peaked and unsteady. The ceiling was so steep Jon bent his head as they entered his attic room. It seemed more like a crawl space, but the necessities were there: a comfortable daybed—she was pleased to see that he had made it—and a blue swivel rocker that looked too small for his gangly body. A hot plate balanced on the windowsill, a phone sat askew on his computer desk, a notepad for doodling beside it. Several of his photos hung on the walls and two pictures sat on the bookcase.

She let her eyes stray the full length of the room again, and then, walking to the narrow east window, pointed beyond the golf course. ''I live over there, near the eighteenth hole.''

He came up behind her. ''I know. When I'm missing you I stand here and imagine us being together.''

His words touched her heart. She had done the same thing, standing in her room at night, staring out at the sky, thinking of him. But she wasn't ready to admit that yet. She turned to the picture on the bookcase of a pretty young woman with red hair. ''But you keep nice company,'' she teased.

''That's Jenna. It's the only picture I have of her.''

''I'm sorry. She was lovely.''

''That's why she caught my attention. I loved her, Tobby.''

Tobin picked up the other frame of a smiling child with wide dark eyes and reddish-brown curly hair. Without looking up, she asked, ''Yours, Jon?''

''I wish. Angelo is eight—an orphan. I support him.''

''He's sweet. Where is he?''

''In the Cotswolds in England. A friend there takes care of waifs, mine included.'' His shoulder brushed hers and he faced her. ''The person who gets me, Tobby, gets the whole package. I'm committed to providing a home for Angelo someday.''

''You never mentioned him before.''

''I've been waiting for the right time. I met Angelo on an assignment in Bosnia during the war there.

Nothing but a little tyke dodging bombs and bullets. He screamed when I picked him up. That's when I realized his wounds were inside."

He took Angelo's picture from her and put it down again. "I smuggled him out of Bosnia when I learned he had no one left alive. After that it took a lot of paperwork to keep him in England."

"Then he's not your son—or Jenna's."

"I want him to be mine. If I can ever plow through the legality, I can give him my name. I think of him as Angelo Woodward. He was just a small fry cowering in the corner of a bombed-out shelter when I picked him up. He didn't know who he was and the only people around him said his family had been killed. He was like a little angel unaware. That's why I called him Angelo."

"I want to meet him someday, Jon."

"You will if you study abroad next year. You'll like him. Right now, he's safe and well-cared for by a motherly woman." He ran his thumb across Tobin's lips. "Tobby, I know who the skipper was referring to today. The girl..."

She fought the urge to cry again and asked softly, "Is she someone you've gone with? I would hate that kind of competition."

"She's an old friend. I've known her since she was ten years old. I'm on standby—there if she needs me. She's been going through some tough times. Once she works those out, I can try and explain that there is someone else in my life...you, Tobby."

He smiled down at her. "Tobby, Jenna was the only other girl for me. I was afraid of the same thing happening again, of losing you like I lost Jenna. I think it's time I told you about her, too. Then you'll understand why I have not wanted to rush in—why I have not risked talking about marriage.''

His voice broke twice as he told her about meeting Jenna in Brussels, of their whirlwind courtship, of following her through Europe, of joining her in a photo shoot in a refugee camp in Africa, of proposing to her on an airplane three months later.

''She called me from Munich to tell me about the baby. I told her to catch the next plane and meet me in London. Tobby, she was a beautiful girl, full of life and laughter and better with the camera than I will ever be. I loved her from the day I met her—and my world fell apart when she died.''

Chapter Seven

Tobin felt Jon's fingers press gently into her shoulders. "Tobby, Jenna was eight years ago. You're now."

He looked down at her, his gaze misty but steady. "Until I saw you at your grandfather's newspaper office, I didn't think I would ever risk loving someone again. Losing Jenna was brutal. But now, wit you—"

Jon abruptly released her, then sat down on the edge of the daybed. He turned toward her, his face chalk-white, and reached out to lock his fingers with hers.

"Oh, Tobby. Just sit with me for a while."

She sat down beside him, taking his hand in both of her own. "You still look sick."

"I am. My feet are like rubber and my gut feels like I'm still riding the ocean waves."

So does mine, she thought. All I can think about is you, about wanting to be with you.

"Tobby, I want nothing more than to take you in my arms. But I don't even have the strength...and I'm scheduled to go out to sea with you again in two weeks. I'll never make it."

She laughed. "Maybe you'll get your sea legs by then."

He rubbed his eyes. "It will take longer than that."

"Then you better not board the *SeaGull* again. But on the next run, we'll stay closer to shore. We're scheduled to check out the habitat of sea lions."

"I can't work up much enthusiasm for that even when I want to be with you as often as I can."

She was on her feet, picking up her purse. "I'd better go before your boarding lady comes back. I don't think she goes to our church, but it would be disastrous if she does."

"Why?"

She cupped her thumbs to her eyes like binoculars. "The elders are watching our every move and making it tough on Dad."

His eyes flashed. "No wonder I don't like church."

"It would be better if you did. Then the elders wouldn't wonder what we were up to. And Dad wants you to come to dinner again. Will you come next Sunday?"

"Will your grandfather be there?"

"He loves pot roast, and that's the usual Sunday menu."

"Give me some time to mull that invitation over. Thanks for getting me home, Tobby. I think I'll just shower and head straight to bed. Will I see you tomorrow?"

"You've forgotten? My friend Jade wants to go mountain climbing with us."

He turned pensive, window-staring. "I think I'll skip the hike tomorrow. That will give you more time with Jade. You wouldn't mind, would you?"

"I'd mind, but it's okay. You may need to rest up tomorrow, anyway." Tobin leaned down and kissed him softly on the forehead. "Get better soon," she whispered. "I'll be studying at the library Monday evening."

"That's a date." He grabbed her hand and placed her palm against his lips. "I think I'm falling in love with you, Tobin."

"Don't tell me that. Not right now." She glanced around his attic room. Neat. Compact. Masculine. Tiny windows looked out on the front lawn, the others on the golf course. "I want us to be together... somewhere romantic when you tell me that."

He didn't let go of her hand. "We are together."

"But I want it to be moonlight and roses. Or maybe a nice candlelit dinner for two. Oh, Jon, I don't want to be dressed like this."

She ballooned the front of her sweatshirt and broke off a loose thread from her cutaway shorts.

"Tobin, I wanted to tell you when we reached the top of the mountain trail last Sunday. But it was too soon. Too scary."

"That would have been a good place. On top of the world."

He shook his head and glanced around his attic room. "And I wanted to tell you when we were out on the *SeaGull*."

"Yes, that would have been a perfect place in the middle of a cerulean-blue ocean. But you avoided me the whole trip."

"I kept stealing glances at you as we approached Newman Island. There we were on opposite sides of the *SeaGull* skimming the water under a cloudless sky. And me seasick."

"So you did notice me?"

"Of course. You with a sunburned nose and that funny wet suit going down the ladder and disappearing beneath the surface. Then you came up from the ocean depths with that straggly wet hair and that crazy outfit. Black flippers in your hand."

"Looking like a drowned rat."

"I thought you were beautiful, Tobby."

"How could you? You were hanging over the rail."

She kissed him again, on the cheekbone this time, and moved her lips along his stubbly jaw. "I think I'd better go and work on my thesis."

"Serious stuff. How will you keep your mind on that?"

"I'll just shift gears the minute I leave you."

"Bet you can't do it."

"I have to go. I'll see you later, Jon. Get some rest."

He was already stretched out on the daybed, his arm covering his eyes, by the time she reached the door. "I love you, Tobin," he mumbled as she doused the light.

Her heart raced and her spirit soared as she ran down the narrow attic steps. Jon loved her. He truly did. She hadn't imagined the words, though it seemed like a dream come true. But so soon some of the exhilaration left her. Her parents would never share her happiness, not if Jon continued to be a stranger to the church. She took the rest of the steps arguing with herself. *How can something so right for me be so wrong?*

On the lower landing she collided with the university quarterback. He grabbed her arms, breaking her fall.

"Well," Wally exclaimed. "Who let you in?"

She felt sudden guilt for no reason at all, mortified, flustered by his mocking grin. She gave a fleeting thought to the church and the deacons and worse, to her father. She was in a hard place; living in Auburn had always been a hard place. But this time she was between the front door and the stairs of Jon's boardinghouse, her escape blocked by a muscular six-footer with a varsity sweater slung over one shoulder.

"Oh, you're Jade Wellington's friend. I met you in Professor Woodward's classroom." She tried to walk around him. "Why the hurry? Is the professor sending you away so you won't break the house rules?"

She rationalized her embarrassment, knowing that it would not have taken much to persuade her to stay. Breaking house rules. Compromising her own convictions. Risking solitary moments with Jon because she wanted to be with no one else.

Wally's eyes traced the staircase to the top and then settled on her again. "Prof Woodward, eh?"

"He's sick. I drove him home from Birchport Harbor."

"Sick? You're the one who looks flushed. You have crimson on your face, Michelson." He brushed at her cheek. "Permanent coloring. You and the professor, eh? You're lucky my aunt isn't home. She has a rule about women on board."

"That's where we were, Wally. On board the *SeaGull*. We hit some rough waters coming back from Newman Island."

"What did you catch out there?"

"A few shellfish." *And some samples of mud like you're slinging at me now.*

He laughed. "What was the professor doing on board?"

"Taking pictures, what else? Please, Wally, I have to go."

With a shrug he stepped aside to let her pass. "Come again if you can take the risk. Just make certain my aunt is out."

She glanced back at him. "Your aunt, Wally?"

"The keeper of the keys." He dangled his own. "She owns this boardinghouse. Sets the rules. Why, the only female who enters the premises beside Aunt Biddy is Jade Wellington."

Tobin's stomach turned to icicles. A pretty young woman with blond hair, the captain had said. Jade! Pretty. Blond. For a moment Tobin couldn't take another step.

"Jade? Jade Wellington here in the boardinghouse?"

"She lives down the street. Pops in every Saturday to cut our hair."

She remembered Jade's business card. *Jade's Cuts and Styling. By appointment only.* Tobin felt sick.

"She's got my aunt wrapped around her little finger."

And what about Jon Woodward? Tobin thought as she fled across the tiled entryway. Does she come at your invitation, Wally, or does she come because Jon Woodward invited her here?

It was eight when Tobin reached the parsonage. As she stumbled up the darkened porch steps, a man stepped from the shadows.

"Who's there?" she cried. Her heart pounded. "You scared me to death, Kedrick."

"If you spent more time with me then you'd recognize me."

His words slurred. Even in the night air she caught the whiff of his breath. "You've been drinking, Kedrick."

"Surprised?"

"Don't, please. You've got to get help."

"You sound like the old man."

She touched his upper arm, gently, as she used to do when she wanted to convince him of something important. "You've never called him that before, Kedrick."

"I do now. He won't get off my back. Thinks if he prays for me all the time, I'll walk the straight and narrow. Sis, do you know how hard it is to walk the straight and narrow in Auburn?"

She nodded in the darkness, knowing. "It's cold out here. We'd better go inside, Ked."

"Can't. Lost my key."

She took her own and opened the door to let them in. Dropping her purse on the nearest chair, she said, "I'll make you some coffee. Then we can sit down and talk."

In the kitchen light, she studied that dear familiar face. His face seemed thinner, the dark brows shadowing the blue of his eyes. His hair was as thick as her own, neatly combed back with only a few loose strands lying limply above the scar on his forehead. She tried to recall that day at the beach, chasing Kedrick across the sand on their eighth birthday. He had grabbed her bucket and shovel and dashed off, with Tobin in hot pursuit.

When he fell, it was right down on the tip of the plastic shovel. She could remember the look on his face when she helped him up and he turned to face her. His wound was bleeding, but something inside him was bleeding more when he said accusingly, "I thought we were friends, Tobby. Why did you hurt me?"

She had been punished for chasing him, hurting him.

It had been that way all their lives. Close one minute. Distant the next. She had envied his good looks, his casual way with the girls, who always found him attractive, desirable.

In high school they had run against each other for class president. And when he won with vicious campaigning, she had cried and said, "Kedrick, I thought we were friends."

"What are you thinking about, sis?" he asked her now.

"About us being kids."

His bottom lip dropped. "We were happy then, weren't we?"

"Usually—except when you beat me for class president."

He grinned, but there was no laughter in his eyes. "I ran against you because I wanted Dad to notice me. You always excelled at everything, Tobby. Just once I wanted to beat you."

"But three weeks after you won, you quit."

"I wasn't any good at something like that. You were always the best, the smartest. I figured if I quit, the kids would never know I couldn't make it."

"I would have helped you—if you had only asked me."

"You never needed me. Look at you—in graduate school. I barely made it through my junior year at the university."

She reached across and patted his arm. "You can do anything you set your mind to. Dad always said that to both of us."

"But I've never known what I wanted to be."

She poured a cup of coffee and inched it toward him. He took a quick gulp. "Gramps wants me to take over the newspaper. I can never do that without you, Tobby. And Dad wants me to fill his spot behind the pulpit. The very thought makes me sick."

What happened to that innocent boyishness? To the kid who had memorized more Bible verses than anyone else in the church? "I always thought you'd grow up to be a preacher," she said.

"The fifth generation of Michelsons behind the pulpit?" he scoffed. "It's got to stop somewhere."

"You used to talk about it."

"To please Dad. That's why I hid all those Bible verses back in my brain cells."

"You were supposed to hide them in your heart."

He tapped his chest. "It's pretty stony in there. Not much room for all that good stuff."

The room filled with Kedrick's unhappiness. She should talk to him—try to help him, but all she could say was, "I've let you down, haven't I, Ked?"

"When you moved away five years ago, my life got off course. I fell apart, sis. You were always the one who believed in me."

"I still do, but I'm going away again next year."

"With Woodward?"

"I don't know," she said honestly. "I might be going east for my doctoral studies. Why don't you go with me, Ked? We can find an apartment together. You can get back on your feet—"

"I can't sponge on you, sis. I have to make it on my own. Besides, I have a feeling that you just might move to Europe."

"With Jon? Then come with us."

She saw the emptiness in his eyes now and ached for him. Always before they had been a transparent blue. Pellucid. Lucid. Clear as crystal. So much more brilliant than her own. No one ever looked at Kedrick without noticing his eyes. All he had to do through high school and the university was to look at a pretty girl and she was smitten, drawn to him by that be-witching gaze.

Softly she asked, "Kedrick, what do you want to do with the rest of your life?"

"To be like you. To succeed. To have people like me."

"But they do. They always have."

"Not according to Brent Carlson. When he stopped me for speeding the last time, he told me that I'd made a drunken mess out of my life—disgraced my family. He said I would ruin your life if you stayed in Auburn. That if I ever took over the paper I'd bring the business crashing down on Gramps's head."

"How dare he!"

"He meant well," he added bitterly. "Don't they all? Brent said he's worried that someday I'm going to blow it and hurt someone I really like."

"Don't listen to him."

He lifted his chin and met her gaze across the table. "Lately, Brent Carlson is about the only one who can talk to me straight on. I think that guy actually cares what happens to me."

"Gramps always idolized you. You were always his favorite."

"I keep letting him down."

"Dad believes in you."

"Not anymore, sis."

"Mom thinks you can do no wrong."

"I know. But I always got in enough trouble for both of us and let you take the rap. It was the easy way out for me."

"What about a girlfriend, Ked? Someone special. Isn't there someone special in your life?"

"I met a girl the other day—someone I could really like. If she'd let me."

"Kedrick, I'm always here for you. You know that."

He scraped back his chair and stood. "Yeah, you'll be somewhere in the world. We'll keep in touch."

He was gone, running unsteadily down the steps, back to his apartment in the basement. She heard the door slam, and waited for the volume of his rock music to blast her even from where she sat, staring emptily into yesterday. What had happened to those days of their childhood when life had been simple, happy?

Chapter Eight

Jon arrived late at the library on Monday evening. When he came he hesitated by the librarian's desk, as though he were searching for Tobin. She caught his eye and he smiled, but there was a sadness in his eyes as he came to her.

"Jon, is something wrong? Is Angelo all right?"

He nodded on both counts as he slipped his arm around her shoulders. She looked up, brushed the unruly lock of hair from his forehead and searched the face she had come to love.

He caught her fingers, kissed them. Then he put what was surely another one of his love notes in front of her. She opened it and stared in dismay. "Tobby," it read, "for now we have to stop seeing each other. I need space. You need space."

"But on Saturday—Jon, we have to talk," she whispered.

He squeezed her shoulder. "Don't make it any harder."

"What changed your mind? What happened?"

"You happened to me," he said softly in her ear. "But I've had some time to think. It's too fast. I'm not the kind of guy that your family wants."

"I don't care what my family wants, Jon."

"Tobby, I want to measure up. Give me time to work it out."

The muscles in her neck felt like cords. She grabbed her pen and wrote, "Good. I've been needing to concentrate on my studies."

As he turned and walked away she crumpled the note and grabbed her books. She shoved them into her briefcase and rushed from the library as the burning-hot tears fell.

For the next two weeks Tobin saw little of Jon, yet as the days passed an unusual calm washed over her. Whatever happened, she knew it would be for the best. She needed time to weigh her own emotions, to lay them out in a row. She had fallen deeply in love, and quickly, and he had cut her off by asking for space.

Okay, Jon Woodward, you can have all the space you want.

It was a false bravado. She missed him and wanted to be with him. But her practical nature took over. As a scientist, she spent hours considering problems and working out the solutions. She jotted the problems down: Europe or a Ph.D.; a successful career or marriage; independence or motherhood to a Bosnian child she had never seen; family commitment or Jon; family approval or Jon. God's best or her own desires?

Jon was right. They needed space. She wanted him

to have a chance to step back as she was doing, to check his own emotions, to know in his heart whether he could really love someone again. Oddly enough, the separation that Jon suggested did not exclude the telephone. They talked on the phone, he mostly from his cell phone, she from hers. Whenever she heard his voice, she pictured him with the deep laugh lines around his hazel eyes. Once or twice she reached out, wanting to touch his cheek, or to run her fingers over his chin, only to realize that she rode in an empty car with a cellular phone in her hand.

Each time he told her he missed her. He missed spending the evenings with her in the library, longed for another mountain trip on Sunday. She wanted to say, *You know where the library is.* Or *Just pick me up after church on Sunday.*

She rode through the city of Auburn, forgetting to turn off on the street to the parsonage. Jon was the most animated when he spoke of Angelo—the slow progress in the courts, the sound of the child's voice long distance from England. She heard the ache that must surely fester within Jon. She tried to picture him as a father and knew that he would make a good one.

In the agreed-upon absence, Tobby willed herself to let him go if it came to that. It was her own time of reflection, setting her priorities right, getting up an hour earlier to walk alone over the campus walkways. She did a lot of heart communing as she walked on what she called her Emmaus Road. She prayed for Jon, prayed that whatever decision he made would make him happy. She confessed her love for him, even wept over it as she tried to compartmentalize that large hunk of herself that thought only of Jon.

Oh, God, even if he leaves Auburn without me, don't let him go without making a choice regarding eternal matters. And don't let him leave without saying goodbye to me.

That evening's phone call was different. Tobin was home early, curled up in a chair in the living room, ignoring her schoolbooks. The ring of the phone almost blasted her from the chair.

Gramps's booming, blustery voice almost burst her eardrum.

"You sitting down, Peanuts?"

She held the receiver away from her ear. "Yes, Gramps."

"I saw you come into my office earlier today. What sent you scurrying out of here without talking to me?"

She was always honest with her grandfather. "I saw Jon."

"All the more reason to come on in and talk. You two can't work out this crazy truce of yours without getting together."

"Jon's choice," she said.

"Humph! Jon said you agreed to it. If you put two and two together, you'd know this was your father's influence. Poor Ross will never think any man is good enough for you. No matter now," he told her. "I have someone here who wants to talk to you."

She had a sinking feeling. Please, not Brent Carlson?

"Well, aren't you going to ask me who's here?"

"I thought you'd tell me, Gramps."

"Are you going to the university's fund-raising dinner?"

"Not without an escort. Besides, that's by invitation only."

"I got you one."

She could hear the mumble of male voices on the other end and then that familiar voice. "Tobby, it's Jon. I've been kicking myself for two weeks. I don't know what got into me. I miss you."

Behind him she heard her grandfather urging, "Get to the point, boy, before she hangs up on you."

"Tobby, will you go to the university dinner with me?"

She gripped the phone with both hands, her small finger tangling in the cord. "I don't think students can attend."

"You can with me. You told me once you wanted a real date—me at the parsonage door with flowers in my hand. I'll make it the biggest corsage I can find. Will you go with me, Tobby?"

"Then you don't need space any longer? You're not going to back off because of my dad?"

"We'll talk about that later. Right now, I just want to be with you."

Tobin spent Saturday afternoon getting ready for the evening. She soaked in a hot bubble bath, did her nails twice, redid her hair, then slipped into her new cocktail dress. She had just snapped her pearls in place when the doorbell rang.

She hovered by the upstairs railing as her father

opened the parsonage door. "Come in," Ross said formally.

She looked down on a smiling man, looking striking in a black tuxedo, a corsage box in his hands. Jon, even dressed in his finery, still had that unruly lock of hair cascading over his brow.

Nervously he said, "I'm here for Tobin."

"So I gathered." Her father nodded toward Tobin, who was making her way down to them. She paused midlanding. "Hi, Jon."

"Tobby! I'd forgotten how beautiful you were," he said as he stepped forward and took her hand.

She felt beautiful in her sleek black dress, but mostly she felt beautiful because Jon was back in her life, if only for this evening. "My folks are going to the same dinner," she warned him.

Ross smiled pleasantly. "It's all right, Mr. Woodward. I've had strict orders from my father-in-law to get to know you better, but this evening we'll go in separate cars. Wini tells me everyone in Auburn who is someone will be there brushing shoulders."

"That's all right, sir. Tobby and I won't even notice them."

They drove forty miles out of Auburn to the exclusive Marco Restaurant with Jon holding her hand all the way.

Inside the brilliantly lit room, the waiter led them to the head table. "What are we doing here, Jon?" she asked.

"I'm one of the guests. You told me once that you wanted the whole world to see us together. I hope the best society of Auburn will do. I like to oblige," he teased, his eyes twinkling.

"But this is ridiculous."

She glanced around the crowded ballroom at the dining tables, filled with china and crystal goblets. Candles flickered on each table. "Why are we at the head table?" she whispered as he held her chair for her.

"They think I'm famous. Your grandfather's doing, I'm sure. I gather he gives a sizable gift annually."

"Yes, he believes in higher education."

"He believes in photojournalists who have traveled abroad."

"Yes, like he wanted to do."

After a dinner of roast duckling and flaming baked Alaska, the university president introduced Jon, boasting about his accomplishments abroad and the photography books that made him a legend. Jon stood behind the podium and spoke movingly about his experiences in Bosnia, Ireland and Africa. He had the audience in his hand, making them laugh one moment, tear up the next. He ended by telling them about Angelo, and before Tobin realized what he was saying, he introduced her as his special guest.

"Many of you know Miss Michelson," he said. "I've been trying to convince her that she would enjoy living abroad. I am certain that Angelo would love to meet her."

And after that—after thunderous applause—the band began to play the songs of the fifties. And she was in Jon's arms, dancing, feeling safe and secure as he swept her across the ballroom and led her out onto the balcony.

"I'll freeze out here," she whispered.

Gallantly he swooped off his dinner jacket and wrapped it around her shoulders.

"Don't crush my corsage."

"Wouldn't think of it."

He remained silent for a moment as they stood by the railing. "K.T. thinks it was your father who forced me to back off. But I owe you an explanation. An apology. I wanted space, Tobin, because I didn't know what kind of life I could offer you. Or whether I dared ask you to be part of it."

He stood very close, his hands gently on her arms. "The truth is, I can't think of life without you, Tobin. Yet right now, I can't make a permanent commitment to you."

"Jenna?" She was surprised at the calm in her voice.

"No, I told you. That's in the past. You're now. But there are other things I have to work out. The kind of life I offer is an unstable one. I travel constantly."

"From the way they talked about you in there, it has been an extraordinary life. One to be proud of."

"There've been mistakes. I don't want to make another one."

Meaning me? she wondered.

The moon was high and full, the stars brilliant, the evening air nippy. Lights from the ballroom filled the archway and yet they were alone on the balcony, a world away from everyone else.

"Tobby, last evening I told Angelo I want to marry you."

"But you haven't asked me yet."

"I have things to settle first," he persisted. "Will you trust me? Will you wait for me?"

"How long?" she asked.

"I wish I knew."

The band was still playing. People dancing. The lights soft in the ballroom. "Let's get away from here, Tobby, and go to the beach?"

"You hate water."

"Not with the moon on it."

"We're not dressed for the occasion."

"We could kick off our shoes and walk along the surf."

"No need," she said. "We're already together."

She touched his chin with a slender finger, felt his face coming closer to hers. The dinner jacket slipped from her shoulders as his warm lips met hers and lingered tenderly.

Chapter Nine

Kedrick was Tobin's first interruption in her Monday-morning rush. She had bounded down the stairs and stopped in the parquet entryway, surprised to see him sprawled on the sofa, scarfing down syrupy waffles.

Eating on the living-room furniture was a no-no with their mother. "Kedrick, get back to the kitchen."

"More comfortable here." He shoved in another bite.

"Don't let Mother catch you."

"She won't argue with me. With Mom I can do no wrong." As he glanced up, scowling, his fork tumbled to the floor and left syrup drippings on the plush carpet.

"Look what you've done. I'll go get the spot remover."

"Don't bother." He snatched the fork from the floor and spread the stickiness with the sole of his shiny shoe. "With you and Dad and that miserable elder board I can do nothing right."

She looked down at the plate still swimming in syrup, at the fork dripping with it. "You need protein."

"I like waffles."

"Come on, I'll make us both some eggs. Then we can start this morning all over."

"You can. I won't. I'm just getting over a splitting headache." He rose and sauntered by her. "I'll have another waffle to go with my eggs. Think you can handle that, Tobby?"

When they reached the kitchen, she sighed wearily as she took his dirty plate and set it to soak. "If your brain isn't swimming in alcohol, it's drowned in sugar."

"Since when did you turn into a health nut?"

She slapped the pan on the stove top and turned to face him. "Since I saw what you were eating."

"Let's not quarrel, Tobby."

"Dad always said we were good at it."

"But you always win."

Was that how he viewed it? He stared back at her now, his blue-green eyes without feeling, not a speck of warmth in them. What had happened between them, between her and this twin brother of hers that she had always idolized, defended, enjoyed? She wanted to reach out and brush the chip from his shoulder.

"You're up early," she said, cracking the eggs.

"Had to see you. I need your car today."

A third egg sizzled in the pan. Calmly she said, "Sorry, I need it myself."

"Come on, sis, I'll drop you off at the university."

"When are you getting your own car out of hock?"

The chair scraped against the white tiles as he sat down. "I need another eight hundred to do that."

Stay calm, she told herself. Don't try to reason with him. "What's wrong with your insurance company, Ked?"

"I didn't turn it in to them." He was whining now, defending himself. "Don't you understand? They would hang me out to dry. I'd have to drive without insurance."

Alarmed, she said, "Then it was more than a fender bender?"

"No other cars were involved. Just mine. A tree trunk wrapped itself around the front end of my car."

"It was your axle the last time. Another tree."

"There's a whole forest out there, especially at night."

"You were drinking," she accused.

"Come on, sis. Don't sound like Dad. It was only a beer or two."

"Two more than you need."

She put down a clean plate with the eggs and another waffle on it. "When are you going to grow up?"

"If I get much taller, you'll have to look up to me."

"You know what I mean. You've got to get a hold on your life, Ked. Even Jon is worried about you. He says you have to accept responsibility."

His face clouded. "I thought Jon and I were hitting it off."

"You did on Saturday. He says you're a good photographer. That you could go places with your talent."

"As long as it's out of Auburn." He licked his fork. "Thanks for inviting me. I haven't been hiking like that for ages."

She started to say he'd held them back, but bit her tongue. He had winded on the trail. But he'd stayed with them all the way to the top. "You should go with us again," she invited.

"I don't want to interfere."

"Oh, Kedrick, we've spent a lifetime doing things together."

"I miss those times," he said moodily. "But don't worry about me, sis. I'm getting it all together. So what about the car? I can't get the pictures Gramps wants without wheels."

"Ask Gramps to stake you to a rental car."

"He bailed me out the last two times."

The eggs in Tobin's mouth were tasteless. "The answer is still no. I need my car. I'm going out to dinner this evening. "

"Woodward again? Not another moonlight and roses?"

She blushed. "No, with my friend Jade Wellington."

"She was wondering when you'd have more time for her."

"I didn't realize you knew Jade so well."

"Yep. She's one good-looking gal."

"Is that all you ever see in a woman?"

He poured on more syrup until his waffle and eggs swam together. "It does get one's attention. Besides, we can blame it on Gramps. He's the one who put me on to her."

She bridled. "Gramps knows her? Why did he introduce you?"

"He sent me out to the campus pool on a photo shoot—Jade Wellington at practice. And she looks good in a swimsuit, too."

"Stop it, Kedrick."

"I'm serious. Haven't you seen her swim? I go to all her meets now. She's fantastic in the water." Excitedly, he said, "Her coach expects her to take them all the way to state championship. Even farther."

She looked at him sharply, wondering whether he was telling the truth. "I didn't notice anything in the *City Herald*."

"Gramps is doing an article on her this Sunday."

"With your photos?"

"Yep, I even checked them out with Miss Wellington." For a moment he seemed guileless, genuine. His full lips parted slightly. "I get a lot of nice perks as the sports editor. I think Jade Wellington is going to be one of them."

"Please, Kedrick, leave her alone. She's a nice gal."

"Nice? Then how come she's divorced?"

Divorced? Jade? "Whoever told you that?"

"She did after the interview—when we had coffee together."

"You hate coffee."

"I'd drink mud to be with a girl like that."

"Ked, if she's been divorced, leave her alone."

"Nice people divorce. But don't let Dad get wind of it when you bring her to the parsonage. He's touchy about things lately. He'd chew you apart for having a divorcée for your best friend."

He was pitting her between her dad and himself—slyly sending his darts at her to split the family even more. "You make Dad out to be such an ogre. He's always liked our friends."

Defiantly he said, "Yours, maybe. Not mine. He told me to keep Kip and Casey away from here. And when I convince Jade to date me, Dad will have ten cat fits."

"Then leave her alone."

"Tobby, you choose your friends. I'll choose mine."

While she was vulnerable, worried, he said, "Can't you ask Jade to take her car this evening? Then I can have yours."

"Kedrick, mine is not on loan anymore. I don't want my car in an accident. I don't want you hurt or hurting someone else."

"I'm careful. I'm walking on lily pads."

The boy who was always careful. Always in trouble. The grown man still taking chances. Running on the edge. "If you're not fit to drive, call me, I'll come and get you."

"That's what your friend Brent Carlson told me."

"You saw him?"

"Yeah. I was driving one of the *City Herald* trucks Friday."

"And he stopped you for speeding?"

"He just gave me a warning this time."

"Thank goodness."

"He wants to know what you're doing this coming Friday."

"Me? I have no idea."

"He wants you to keep it free."

She was keeping it free for Jon Woodward. She stacked the dirty dishes and headed for the sink, the salt-and-pepper shakers in her apron pocket. "If Brent Carlson wants to see me, have him call like a proper gentleman."

"He calls often. Mom tells him you're busy." His smirk widened. "Can't remember whether she mentioned Jon Woodward or not."

Kedrick remained in his chair, his eyes mocking as he watched her. She wiped the table and then turned to the sink and plunged her hands into the hot, sudsy water. Her fingers were still sudsy when the wall phone beside Kedrick rang.

On the fifth ring, when it was obvious that Kedrick intended to ignore it, she reached across him and snatched the receiver. "It's all right, Dad. I picked it up down here." And then, her voice still agitated, "Hello, Michelsons' residence."

"Tobin?" Her grandfather's deep baritone roared over the line. She held the receiver an inch from her ear as he said, "You tell that scalawag of a brother of yours to get down to the office. Now. He was due an hour ago." Gramps sounded short of breath. "I'm not running some toy-shop operation. We've a paper to get out today."

"Do you want to talk to him, Gramps?"

"Just give him my message."

The phone on the other end slammed in Tobin's ear. "It was for you, Kedrick. You'd better get down to the *Herald* now."

He stood, stretched lazily and mumbled a false apology. "Sorry that you caught that one, Tobby."

"I usually catch the brunt of your mistakes."

"That's what twins are for. They live in the buffer zone." He shoved his chair back in place. "You heard Gramps. He wants me down there pronto. I need your car, Tobby."

"No, you drive too recklessly."

His hand tightened on the chair back. "Then can you give me a lift?"

"That will only make me late for class. When is that van of yours coming out of the shop?"

"I told you—when I come up with another eight hundred dollars."

Tobin reached Jade's tiny apartment shortly after six that evening. It was a compact little place, neat as a pin and full of the bright colors that Jade liked, from the throw pillows on the sofa to the blue-green seascapes that hung on the wall. A Spanish beat on the stereo vibrated the walls.

"I hope I'm not late," Tobin shouted above the music. "I stopped off at the store to buy you some candy."

"Caramels! Good," Jade said, tearing the wrapping free.

"Don't spoil your dinner with candy."

"I'm just satisfying my sweet tooth. You can take the grand tour—it will take you all of ten seconds—and then come on out to the kitchen. I'm putting the finishing touches to our meal."

She licked the caramel from her finger and waved Tobin toward the bedroom. As Tobin passed the stereo she lowered the volume, then went into Jade's room where a fancy patchwork quilt served as a bed-spread. Jade's camera and textbooks were sprawled on top. Photos graced the top of the dresser along with a single snapshot of Jade with a young man. Had that been her husband?

Tobin went back through the living room and into the kitchen, where the table was set for two. A salad bowl was heaped to the top, and the crystal goblets crackled with ice water.

"That's my version of the house salad," Jade said. "As many vegetables as I can squeeze into it."

"Looks good."

"I won't be long, Tobin." She slipped her hand into an oven mitt before lowering the oven door.

"Smells delicious."

"We'll know in a few minutes. Hope you like lasagna from scratch and fresh asparagus."

Tobin sniffed again. "We'll know in a few minutes."

They were still laughing as they dug in. Halfway through the meal Tobin said, "You're a great cook, Jade."

"I stick with six recipes and that's it."

"You've changed," Tobin said when Jade brought out two thick slices of lemon sponge cake.

"I hope so. It's been ten or twelve years since Running Springs. I hated setting tables and getting stuck on KP duty."

"That's not it. I'm talking about the few weeks since we saw each other again. You're just more mature."

"Yeah. That's me. Really mature. Studying hard."

"You do so much for others. The swim team admires you to the hilt for overcoming asthma and taking them to victory. But you worry me, piling thirty hours into every day. When do you rest?"

"Guess who's talking. You don't sleep much yourself."

"But I hate to see you burning candles on the weekend."

"Swimming is my whole life right now. Something I do well."

"You're really good at anything you do. But you never take time for yourself. You never date anyone, do you?"

"Not anymore." Jade spread the last bite of lasagna in the center of her plate, her eyes downcast, her blond hair falling against her cheek. "The only one I'm interested in is taken."

Tobin squirmed against the warning signal inside. All evening Jade had been bubbly, effervescent, and suddenly her mood had swung. "Someone I know?" she asked Jade.

"Would it matter?"

It would matter if she meant Jon Woodward. Surely she didn't mean Jon. "Jade, my brother told me you were married once."

Her head jerked as she faced Tobin. A flicker of surprise, of sadness, crossed her face. "So you know about that?"

"I didn't know until Kedrick mentioned it."

"I was afraid he'd tell you. It happened six years ago—a high school sweetheart. One of those once-in-a-lifetime forevers. Only, it didn't end up that way. Cory and I called it quits after three years. It took longer for the courts to make it final."

"I'm sorry."

"I'm sorry, too. I really thought I could make a go of it. My parents were heartsick. They didn't like Cory, nor trust him. But I was stubborn. I really thought I could make it work. My folks married young and made a go of it. When you're fresh out of high school, you think you know everything. Can do anything. Tell me, Tobin, does it make a difference? Me being divorced and all?"

"It doesn't to me."

"How about your church? Your father?"

Tobin's pause was too long as she toyed with her sponge cake. "We don't have to tell them. Stir the waters."

"So it will make a difference?"

"I told you—not to me. We were friends at camp, remember? We'll tell Dad that we just picked up from there."

"Yeah, best of friends at Running Springs. That's what I wanted to be, but you didn't have much time for me there."

"I really did blow it back then, but we're friends now."

"I like that—need it," Jade said.

"You? You have lots of friends. You can barely spare me three lunch hours a week or a twenty-minute phone call."

"I know a lot of people," she admitted. "But none of them really know me. They don't know what makes me tick."

"Jade, why don't you have dinner with me over at my parents' home this week? I'll check with Mom about the time."

"At the parsonage? They won't be playing my kind of music."

My brother will, she thought. "Look, my folks are really quite normal," Tobin said, defending them. "Down-to-earth. Homespun people."

"That's not the way your brother describes them."

"His opinions aren't all that reliable lately."

"I don't know. Your dad looked a little intimidating in his preacher's garb on Sunday."

"You were there?"

"In the back row, ducking behind a hymnbook. What was he wearing—that funny thing with puffy sleeves?"

"You mean his clerical robe? It's called a vestment. He's the fourth generation of the Michelsons to wear it."

"Four preachers in your family?"

"They're all dead except Dad."

"Preaching could kill a body, especially the way he got all steamed up on Sunday."

Tobin laughed, seeing her dad in a new light. "So what about dinner at the parsonage, Jade?"

"You'd better check with that brother of yours, too."

Tobin frowned. "What's wrong with Kedrick?"

"He was grumpy the first day I met him. He was trying to get some photos and said I splashed water on his camera."

"Kedrick grows on you."

Above their laughter the chimes in the university towers rang dolefully.

Jade leapt to her feet. "Leave the dishes, I'll catch them later. I have a night class in ancient history. But I'd better cut that tonight," she announced with a twinkle. "I have some haircuts scheduled. I'm the lady barber at the boardinghouse down the street."

"Professor Woodward's boardinghouse?"

"That's the place. It keeps me in lasagna and chewing gum. Why don't you come along?" she teased. "Jon will be there."

Tobin blushed. "Some other time."

"Whatever you say. But if you like the guy, you gotta go for him. If you don't, someone else will."

Did she mean herself? Tobin wondered. Did she have her eye seriously on Jon Woodward? Or were they, as Jon said, just good friends? As they left the apartment and Tobin stepped into her car, Jade sprinted down the narrow path toward the boarding-house, cutting across the neighbor's manicured lawn and through a flower bed.

Chapter Ten

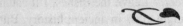

Early in November Ross Michelson sat in his soft leather recliner, his long legs stretched out on the ottoman. The *City Herald*'s sports page with Kedrick's latest action shot lay crumpled on his lap. He turned to watch the young woman who stood with her back to him, her hands locked behind her. With her head tilted back, her cornsilk hair brushed her shoulders.

This was the third time that Jade Wellington had been a guest in his home. He did not like the girl. No, that was not true. He did not trust her, not with Kedrick showing a growing interest in her. Yet at this moment she seemed drawn like a magnet to the painting above the fireplace—Robert Zund's magnificent rendition *On the Road to Emmaus*.

"That picture interests you, Jade."

"Yes," she said without turning. "It fascinates me. It's both sad and beautiful at the same time."

"I find it that way sometimes."

"It's like autumn the way the sunlight is reflecting through the trees. The leaves are like a burnt orange and it's almost a blinding light glowing on the trail where the men are walking."

"It would be like our springtime," he said. "Not autumn."

"But the colors. Look at the colors."

He tried to see it from her eyes—something so familiar to him. The brilliance on the Emmaus Road. The Christ, risen from the tomb, doing what He had always done in His earthly journey—encouraging those who were sad of heart. It represented Easter to Ross, a painting of hope. It had always comforted him.

An ancient tree bent toward the water, its gnarled roots dappled with moss. The faint outline of a village lay ahead, barely in focus. And that magnificent light at the close of day fell on the shrubs and the trees and that dusty trail on the Emmaus Road. But it was more than a sunset that brought light to the painting. It was Christ, who had stepped out of the tomb and was walking along the way. This was what Ross saw, what stirred his heart afresh with each viewing. But what did Jade see?

He leaned forward. "Are you familiar with the painting, Jade?" he asked gently.

She looked at the three men in long robes, one with his feet bare, the others with their feet shod in sandals. "I recognize Jesus, Rev."

Do you? he wondered, but he winced at the name she had called him. Then he wondered, had she done it on purpose, just to nettle him? To play up to some prejudiced image he had of her—of which she was painfully aware.

"The other two are strangers. Were they His disciples?"

"In a way, Jade, but they were weary and sad of heart that day. They thought they were talking to a stranger. The day was far spent, their hearts heavy with thoughts of the crucifixion."

"And they didn't know who He was?"

"They were slow of heart."

"Because they walked with Jesus and didn't know Him?"

"Because He walked beside them, Jade, and they didn't recognize Him. But His footprints are always there."

An embarrassed chuckle burst through her lips. "Slow of heart like I am? Too blind to see the footprints? Is that what you think?"

He wasn't certain what he thought about her. Wasn't sure what she believed. "Jade, if I can be of help," he offered.

She shrugged. "Don't go preachy on me, Reverend."

"No offense intended. But you seem sad today. I thought—well, my daughter tells me you were married once."

She glanced around and met his gaze. "You're not very comfortable with me being divorced, are you, sir?"

"Does it show that much?" he asked. He pressed his temples. "Jade, I've been so unfair to you. I just have a problem with how young people toss marriage aside these days.''

"I didn't toss mine aside. My husband left me. If it's Kedrick that concerns you, you don't have to worry, Mr. Michelson. Kedrick and I are merely friends.''

"Here I am trying to help you and I'm only making it worse.''

"I think I understand your son. He's very troubled, you know. But I think if he understood what was happening in this painting, it would help him.''

"It's been hanging there all his life.''

"But when is the last time he noticed it?''

Ross shook his head. "Lately, it is difficult to know what my son thinks or feels. He hides everything well.''

"Not well.'' She gave another nervous little chuckle. "He's very much like my ex.'' He heard bitterness in her voice. "Kedrick hides behind a bottle. You know that, don't you?''

If she had determined to ward off a sermon, she succeeded. Ross sat straight up, dropping the sports page on the floor by his chair. There was a sadness about Jade Wellington. He had noticed it the first time she entered the church, and had realized it more as she sat at dinner with them. It was not in what she said, for she was charming, her lively conversation interspersed with a contagious chuckle that held Kedrick's interest in her. And yet her laughter did not erase the sadness in her eyes, the pain that she must be bearing—perhaps from her broken marriage.

He eased out of the chair and went to stand beside

her, his own hands locked behind his back, his head bent to gaze at the painting with her. "Jade, it wasn't until Christ broke bread with those men that their eyes were open and they recognized Him."

"You mean they had dinner together?"

"You could call it that. After He left them they realized that their hearts had burned within them when He talked to them."

She put her hand to her chest, covering the emerald necklace that she wore. "I think I know what they meant," she said. "They were walking with Him and didn't even know Him. I'm like that, Mr. Michelson. I'm walking my own Emmaus Road."

"Perhaps my daughter should give you a painting like this for Christmas. I'll suggest it."

"I'd like that. But, Rev, what if I don't make it until Christmas?"

"Are you planning to go somewhere?"

She was thoughtful. "I don't know what made me say that. A premonition, maybe. You'd better tell your daughter my birthday is two weeks before Christmas. Maybe she'd better give me the painting for my birthday."

Ross felt uneasy. "I'll remind Tobin. She plans on having your birthday party here at the parsonage."

Jade's blue eyes lit with amusement. "You wouldn't mind?"

"Not now."

"I'd like that. My last few birthdays were miserable. After my ex and I split...I thought life wasn't worth living. I do now."

"You've had a rough time, haven't you?"

"Haven't we all? You know, Reverend, I didn't like you when I met you. I thought you were kind of arrogant behind the pulpit, as though you thought I wasn't good enough for your church."

He cleared his throat. "I deserved that. I haven't been very gracious to you. Perhaps we can start over."

She glanced at him. "Are you for real?"

"I'd like to be."

"I'm still divorced. Not the kind of person you want around your kids—or influencing the young people of your church."

"I deserved that, too. Can you forgive me, Jade?"

"Yes, I can. I do."

Her attention was drawn back to the painting. "I wish I had seen this picture back when my marriage fell apart. I don't know what it is, Reverend, but something in that picture captures my thoughts. It's as though I want to be there walking with them. Listening to them talk."

"I believe they talked about forgiveness—"

"Don't let the painting turn you on, Jade," Kedrick said from the doorway. "It's just some artist's concept."

She turned on him. "No, you're wrong, Kedrick."

He put up both hands. "Okay. Okay. I won't argue with you. But if you can break away from Dad, I'll challenge you to a game of tennis."

She offered him a radiant smile. "Some other time, Kedrick. Your sister and I are going to visit a friend of mine."

He scowled. "I'd like to meet your friend. Why not now?"

Jade walked across the room to him. She reached out and touched Kedrick's arm. "I'll introduce you someday."

He caught her hand. "Call her. She can play tennis with us."

"She doesn't play tennis anymore, Kedrick. She did once."

From behind them Ross said, "I'd enjoy a game of tennis, Kedrick. What about it, son?"

Kedrick's scowl deepened. "Some other time, Dad."

As Tobin and Jade left the parsonage, Tobin asked, "Your car or mine?"

"We'll take my car, Tobby. I know the way and I don't want to miss the visiting hours at the nursing home."

"I'm sorry I took so long. I was talking to Jon."

"Kedrick said you forget everything when you're with Jon."

"That's my father's line. Jade, I'm sorry. I never meant to feed you to the wolves while I talked on the telephone."

"Actually, we got on fairly well this time. Your dad kept his sermon low-key. We talked about the Emmaus Road mostly."

"The painting in the living room? My grandmother gave it to my parents on their first anniversary. You like it? Jon does, too. Everyone seems to like it but Kedrick."

They were in the car now, backing out of a tight space. "Maybe he's tired of the familiar. I'll ask him the next time we get together."

Alarmed, Tobin said, "You're still getting together with Kedrick? You're not—"

"Dating him? Of course not. I like talking to him. He's such an enigma, but he's a deep thinker."

"I wouldn't exactly call him that."

"Maybe you haven't listened to him lately."

"We had a long talk at the kitchen table three weeks ago."

"That's what we have. Chats over coffee and tea. He's one of my clients. I just didn't tell you."

"You cut Kedrick's hair?"

"Yeah, Professor Woodward told me he needed a good barber. Cuts and styles by Jade. He's easy to do—nice thick hair. Don't look so worried. We're just friends."

"Keep it that way, eh? He's too messed up to get involved."

"Believe me, I plan to stay free—at least for now. Kedrick wanted to come with us today, Tobin."

"To the nursing home?"

"He didn't know where we were going. I thought you'd never get off that telephone and come to my rescue."

"Kedrick is not a very happy camper these days, Jade. But I love him. I've always covered for him, but I'm having a hard time with that now."

Jade glanced in her rearview mirror and said casually, "Because he's drinking?"

Tobin stretched the seat belt, hating the pressure

against her shoulder, hating the way the conversation was going. "I'm sure that's part of it. He's making such a mess of his life."

"He needs you, Tobin."

"That's hard to figure. He keeps pushing me away. Ignoring me. Except the other Saturday when he went hiking with Jon and me. And now he's withdrawn again."

Jade gunned the engine. "Because he's hurting. He said he doesn't have any friends left. Said he was counting on you coming home. And all you do is spend time with Jon or me."

"I did come home. But it wasn't what I wanted. He has a splendid opportunity at the newspaper office as the sports editor and he's ruining that. He's almost twenty-seven and he lives scot-free at home. The only thing he pays is his own telephone bill."

"My ex drank. Drowned himself in sorrows. I don't want to see that happen to Kedrick. That's why I spend time with him. Drive him home so he won't get another fender bender."

"My father won't like that."

"Because I'm divorced? I'm not dating him, Tobin. Just being his friendly hairstylist. He's good at tennis. You know that, don't you?"

"You're playing tennis with him, too?"

"Frequently. Do you have a problem with that, Tobby?"

"Kedrick plays all over the court. I would think that much exertion would be tough on your asthma."

"It's harder than swimming. But Kedrick's good in sports. He plans to go to my swim meet Sunday a week from now. What about you, Tobin? Will you come, too?''

"Jon and I usually go hiking on Sunday afternoons, but I'll ask him.''

Jade slowed the car. "On Sundays? Then I ruined your Sunday together. If you'd rather, we can visit my friend another time.''

"No, I've messed up enough of our get-togethers.''

Fifteen minutes later Jade's car rattled to a stop at the convalescent home, a one-story building sheltered by a six-foot hedge. As they walked into the lobby, it was obvious that Jade knew everyone. She stopped to kiss the cheek of a barefoot man who had left his walker behind and to pat the trembling hand of a wrinkled old woman restrained in a wheelchair. She waved as the nurses greeted her warmly, one of them saying, "Betts has been waiting for you all day.''

"I'm really late. Sorry.''

My fault, Tobin thought, and felt a sense of guilt for talking on the phone so long with Jon.

She followed Jade down the wide corridor and into the end room, expecting to see someone chatty and gray haired, but they stopped at the bedside of a young woman Jade's age. She lay on her back, the linens fresh about her, a bouquet of forget-me-nots on her bedside stand. Her face was pretty, her dark hair brushed to a shine. The girl's eyes were glassy, unmoving, ceiling bound.

Jade squeezed one of the splinted hands, running her fingers over the contractures. "Hi, Betts,'' she said cheerily. "You look so pretty today. And look at you wearing your favorite blouse.''

Jade kept her fingers wrapped around the girl's as she chatted amiably. "I brought a friend to meet you, Betts. Her name's Tobin—like you'd probably say it's an oddball name. But that's her grandfather's fault."

She leaned down. "And that's not all. Her dad's a preacher. I've just been talking to him about the Emmaus Road. I'll tell you about that the next time I come."

She caressed the limp fingers affectionately and winked across the bed at Tobin. "It's okay to talk to her, Tobby. She loves visitors. I come all the time."

Tobin glanced around. "I'm not much into this."

"Sure you are. You talk to shellfish and crayfish all the time. You even have pet names for your sea turtles."

"That's different."

Jade said calmly, "It's tougher when it's a human being."

"Hi, Betts," Tobin managed. She thought about telling her about migratory birds or global changes in the environment. She mumbled something about the tide pools and the Audubon Club and something about vanishing birds and the sea turtle called Dizzy.

"Betts loves animals," Jade said. "Especially robins. Don't you, Betts?"

Tobin was five minutes into the one-sided conversation when she found the courage to run her fingers gently over the back of Betts's hand. Her skin was tissue soft, transparent. She found herself saying, "Betts, I'm a marine biologist. I wish you could see the algae—the seaweed I collect. Some are bright green like your eyes and some are velvety soft like your skin feels to me.''

She looked at Jade and whispered, ''What happened to her?''

''A car wreck six years ago.''

''Six years like this in a coma?''

''Yeah, the man who hit her was picked up on a DUI, but he walked free.''

She understood now. Jade was determined to help Kedrick, to keep him from doing this to someone else.

''Betts was my best friend in high school. Stood up for me when I got married.'' She squeezed the girl's hand again. ''We're still friends. Right, Betts? I'm short on funds so I didn't bring flowers today. But the next time I'm flush, I'll bring you a dozen red roses like the ones in your mom's garden. We have to go now, Betts. But we'll come back soon. At least, I will.''

Back outside, Tobin gulped in the fresh air. ''I realized in there how lucky I am to have a friend like you, Jade. How lucky Kedrick is.''

''You barely know me. We've only been pals for a few weeks.''

''Seems a lot longer than that. They've been good weeks.''

''Me special? Betts is the one who's special. I always feel good about myself when I spend time with her. And I wasn't kidding in there. As soon as I can collect enough extra money cutting hair I'm going to buy her some more red roses.''

''But she wouldn't know they were there.''

"Sure she will, Tobin. I'll let her smell them and feel them."

"You know she doesn't hear you. Doesn't know you're there."

"I think she does. But I never want to be like that, Tobin. Betts was meant to fly, not lie there wasted."

As she slipped into the driver's seat, she added, "If anything like that ever happens to me, Tobin, I want my folks to set me free. To let me go. Promise me you'll tell them that."

Tobin bypassed the lump in her throat and said lightly, "Sure thing. I'll tell them you want to fly like a bird. Right?"

"More like a monarch butterfly. Fragile-winged and beautiful. Something spectacular that comes out of its cocoon like Betts will do some day. I pray that for Betts every day. That she would be free."

"You want to fly," Tobin repeated. "To sprout wings."

"That's the way life was meant to be."

Chapter Eleven

A brisk November breeze cut across the crowded university stadium, blowing candy wrappers and empty paper cups under the bleachers. The autumn wind twisted Tobin's shiny hair and whipped it against her rosy cheeks. She brushed at the long strands, her eyes on Jon Woodward down on the sidelines. His back was to her, his broad shoulders hunched forward as he aimed his camera at the football squad.

Shivering, Tobin pulled the collar of her woolly jacket around her neck. But it wasn't just the cold wind. *It's you, Jon. You didn't call last evening, like you promised. I sat curled on one end of the sofa waiting, hoping, praying that you'd ring me. I imagined what we would say when the phone rang. I could hear the laughter in your voice even in the empty room. I could picture you pushing back those unruly strands of brown hair from your forehead.*

"Hi, sweetheart," you would say.

And even at my age, my heart would have done
flip-flops beating out of control. I wanted you to call.
I fell asleep sitting there with my biology book still
in my hands, my bare feet like ice.

In spite of the numbing weather, Jon was down
there on the field wearing only a thick Shetland
sweater, his broad ungloved hands adjusting the wide-
angle lens. Then in what appeared to be total frustra-
tion, he slapped his thigh. With her attention so intent
on Jon, Tobin had missed the play, but some line-
backer would get the coach's raking at half time.

Right now Tobin didn't know the score. I've been
too busy watching you, Prof Woodward, wondering
whether you'll call me tonight. Wondering whether I
baked those chocolate chip cookies in vain.

She stole a glance at the friend beside her. Jade
held out a half-filled bag of peanuts. Tobin shook her
head. I'd choke on them, she thought. A few weeks
ago she couldn't survive a game without a bag of
peanuts or popcorn.

"You're usually such fun, Tobby. But not lately.
You're getting too much like me—soaring one minute, falling into the pit of despair the next. What's
up? Trouble with your classes?"

"Trouble keeping my mind on them."

Jade nodded toward the playing field. "Woodward,
eh?"

Tobby was glad that her cheeks were already rosy
with the weather. "He's hard to figure out. A female
reporter at the *City Herald* wrote an article on Jon's
career abroad. Did you see it?"

Jade laughed. "She obviously didn't know him, not

when she called him 'a man of granite with the tough hide of an elephant.' She was a bit harsh, don't you think?''

"She was," Tobin agreed. "But I'm afraid Jon rebuffed her at the fund-raising dinner. Maybe that's why she suggested that he was a man to be wary of. 'Lest he leave broken hearts behind him when he leaves Auburn,''' she quoted.

"Don't worry. Woodward lets criticism roll right off him."

But Tobin disliked people criticizing his public image. He was a very private man. A romantic man. But is that all there is for us, Jon Woodward? Nine marvelous weeks of your calls, of late dinners by candlelight at unexpected moments, of long drives roaring along the Pacific cliffs, talking and laughing together. Am I just another interlude in your life? Is that all it meant to you, Prof Woodward? I can dissect frogs or analyze sea lions or dive off the *SeaGull,* but I can't predict or control a relationship with the one person I want more than anything else.

"Jade, I really thought he was going to call me last night," she admitted.

"And he didn't." Jade concentrated on cracking a peanut shell, but her fingers shook as she shelled it. "Maybe he was busy helping a student in need. He's that kind of person, Tobby."

She was trying to read Jade's bland expression when a call echoed through the noisy stadium. "Tobin. *Tobin.*"

Jade nudged her. "I think that's your call to arms," she said, pointing down toward Kedrick.

"Oh, no." Tobin shook her head, losing sight of Jon for the moment. "What does Kedrick want this time?"

Jade shrugged. "He's your brother. I'm glad it's you he wants. But you know he won't give up until you give in."

Kedrick looked as edgy as the wind. These past few weeks they had little in common except their birthday. She turned back to Jade, torn between her brother and her friend. Jade's high cheekbones were chafed in the weather, her flaxen hair wind tossed, her usual bubbly smile frazzled at the sight of Kedrick.

"I have to go, Jade. I'm sorry. Call me this evening."

There was a slight hesitation. "I'm busy."

"Tomorrow, then."

Reluctantly Tobin stood and ran down the steps. "What do you want now?" she asked when she reached Kedrick.

"I want you down there taking pictures for me. You can see everything better down there."

"I had a good seat. But thanks to you, it's gone now."

"You won't need it. You'll be right down there on the sidelines." He nodded toward the fifty-yard line. "Come with me."

She glared up into his face, frightened by the sullen look in his wide eyes. "Kedrick, take your own pictures. Gramps hired you. I won't go down on the football field for you."

"It will put you right down there with lover boy."

"Can't you understand? Jon and I are just good friends."

"I'm not stupid, sis. It was bad enough when he took up all your time, but now he's made friends with Gramps. And where does that leave me? On the outside. But I'm family. I'm your brother. You owe me your loyalty."

She felt a knot of tension in her stomach. "No, Kedrick. I won't go make a fool of myself, not even for you. Jon will think I'm throwing myself at him."

"Well, aren't you?"

No, she told herself, that's not what I'm doing. "I'm not going. I'm tired of covering for you."

"Just this once."

She had heard it a hundred times. Her brother, her twin. She could see now that his eyes were blurry, his hand shaking as he lifted the camera strap over his tousled hair. "Are you all right, Kedrick?"

"Please, Tobin," he urged. "You've got to help me."

"You're the sports editor. It's your job."

His face twisted. "No, it's my neck if I don't get some good shots of this game for Gramps."

"The paper won't fall apart without them."

"But this is the big competition—the pre-Thanksgiving game. Win or lose, Gramps wants good shots of the game."

He held up his unsteady hand. "I'm in no shape to take pictures today. Gramps thinks the coach down there is newsworthy. He's a potential coach for the NFL in the future. Please, Tobin. I can't let Gramps down. I'll meet you after the game."

"Kedrick, I don't have a press card."

He shoved one into her hands. "Use mine. No one will know the difference with names like ours."

Jon will know, she thought. What will I tell him?

"If anyone asks, just tell him you're the sports editor for the *Auburn City Herald*. Woodward is smart enough to keep his mouth shut. He might even help you."

He shook his head and added bitterly, "I don't know why Gramps keeps trying. Nobody cares about a small-town paper that will die when he dies. Most people don't even know that Auburn exists. We're nothing more than a bend in the road forty miles from nowhere. A community of twenty thousand residents. A couple of shopping malls. A few churches and schools."

"And the offices of the *City Herald*," Tobin said. "A lot of people know about the *Herald*. And, Kedrick Michelson, K. T. Reynolds is still a big name in journalism. The paper is our grandfather's pride and joy."

"Nothing more. The whole business will die when he does. You're missing half the game, Sis. If anyone bothers you down there, tell them old man Reynolds sent you."

"That's no way to talk about our grandfather."

Kedrick pressed his fingers into her arm. "It's okay, Tobin. That's what the sports fans still call him. So don't worry."

He urged her down the steps and out on the playing field. "Just be sure you get some good action shots," he called.

She pocketed her gloves and felt the biting wind cut into her fingers as she shouldered the camera and stepped up beside the other photographers. With the uproar in the stadium, she was just part of the scenery as she edged her way toward the sideline, camera poised. She focused aimlessly at first. Then as her nerves settled she ran with the pros, catching a shot or two of action plays on the thirty-yard line. And then she zoomed in on the face of Jon Woodward. She imagined him in Ireland snapping the faces of children. In Bosnia photographing the ravages of war. Or catching the winning play at Wimbledon.

When he spotted her, he smiled. "What are you doing here?"

"Filling in for Kedrick."

"So he's shirking his responsibility again? What a guy."

Jon's attention went back to the game, but at the first time-out, he closed the gap between them. "I'm sorry I didn't have time to call you last night."

"It really didn't matter. Great game," she said.

He shrugged. "They've made some mistakes. Lost some points."

"But they're winning."

The referees were in a huddle, arguing among themselves, trying to come to terms with a question-able call. "Success," he warned, "lasts no longer than the flutter of that camera lens."

"Will I see you after the game, Jon?"

"I'll be busy in the locker room. The coach agreed to let me talk with the players and take some shots."

"And after that?"

He scowled at the coach with the thick mustache who had signaled for another time-out. "I'm busy tonight, Tobin. I'm sorry. I promised to take Jade to dinner."

Her legs went wobbly.

He called back over his shoulder, "She speaks highly of you, Tobin. You've been good for her."

It was several minutes—several plays later—before he turned her way again. "Jon, I didn't know you and Jade were dating."

"We're just having dinner together. We go back a long time."

"To the time when Jade was married?"

"Before that. Jade has ridden a rough road since her divorce."

Walking the Emmaus Road, Tobin thought. Without knowing that the Shepherd was walking beside her. I thought everything was squared away, Jon. I thought we were going steady. That we shared everything. But not you, Jon Woodward. I won't share you.

The noise in the stadium erupted. The teams were charging off the field, the spectators racing onto it. Auburn's final play had slipped past her camera. Kedrick would have fits.

Jon stopped beside her for a second. He knuckled Tobin's cheek. "It's not what you think, Tobby. Jade and I are just good friends and right now that's what Jade needs."

He swiped back a shock of tangled hair, his dark eyes pleading with her, "Trust me, please. What about midnight, Tobby? I'll bring you your favorite doughnuts, glazed, right?"

She smarted. "Jade is the one who likes glazed doughnuts."

His rock-hard shoulders slumped. "Then I'll buy some ice cream. I know *your* favorite is maple nut."

Don't bother, she wanted to say. Not if a date with Jade is more important. But she saw the tired jagged lines around his eyes and wondered what was worrying him. No, she wouldn't give Jon Woodward up that easily, not even to her best friend.

He grabbed the rolls of film from his camera bag. "Take these. You're going down to the *City Herald*, aren't you?"

"Yes, with Kedrick."

"Just in case your shots didn't turn out, take mine."

"I'll tell grandfather—"

He squeezed her hand. "No need to tell him. Just let him use what he needs. I have to go," he said as other reporters pressed in on him. "What about midnight, Tobby?"

"You're not avoiding my father by coming so late?"

"Wouldn't you?"

"I'm sure he'll be in bed."

"Tell him to take his sermons with him. Honest, I've never met a man before who greets you with a sermon instead of a handshake. He should lighten up. He's about scared Jade off from your doorstep. Her faith is fragile enough."

Tobin nodded, unable to voice an apology for her father. Life had never been easy at the parsonage. And now it was getting worse, with her father's visible mistrust of her best friends.

"Don't ring the door when you come. I'll be watching for you. And don't forget the ice cream to go with the chocolate chip cookies I made for you."

"Sounds good." He leaned down and gave the news media something to talk about as he kissed her cheek. "I'll be there, Tobby. Count on it. Pick out some good CDs so we can relax."

She knew that Jon took his music by moods—his CDs an odd mixture of soft rock to blast away his headaches, country western to calm him, romantic songs or Schubert for his evenings alone.

"Should I go back to a Simon and Garfunkel?" she teased.

"Just back to 'Autumn Leaves.'" He stopped yards from her and called back, "How does your father handle being awakened at midnight?"

She blew on her frostbitten fingers. "Not very well."

"Then he wouldn't like what I have to say. Some day I want to talk to him about getting married."

Tobin's heart sank. He wanted to marry Jade. "Maybe you and Jade better make an appointment with him for one of his counseling sessions."

"Jade and me?" He laughed out loud. "Tobby, I want to talk to him about you. You're so old-fashioned, I'll have to ask him for permission to marry you. It's about time I faced up to him, don't you think?"

But Jon wouldn't like it if her father laid down the

ground rules for God being the head of the house. "Not tonight," she warned. "Some other time."

"It's this church thing, isn't it? God always comes between us."

Jon didn't wait for her answer, but ran across the field toward the locker rooms, his lanky legs moving at an even pace. She caught her breath. In spite of the threat of Jade Wellington, Tobin's spongy heart was doing flip-flops again.

Tobin and Kedrick argued all the way to the *City Herald,* but Tobin kept silent when the rolls of film were developed and Kedrick spread them out on their grandfather's desk.

The pictures were good. Great, in fact. She and Gramps leaned over Kedrick's shoulder.

"Humph," he grunted, thumping Kedrick on the back, "you get better all the time, son. One of these days, you'll be able to take over the newspaper." He paused, his bushy brows almost hiding his twinkling eyes. "At least the sports column."

Tobin winced as Gramps picked up Jon Woodward's picture of the winning touchdown. He patted Kedrick's shoulder again. "I've left a spot on the front page for this one. A splendid shot."

Surely Kedrick will tell Gramps the truth, she thought.

Kedrick met her gaze with a sly, twisted grin that broadened innocently for his grandfather. "I was really lucky to get that one," he said.

Chapter Twelve

Tobin humored herself with a long drive along the ocean, and on the way back decided to spin by Jade's place. With any luck, she would find Jade on her own and the two of them could go back to the empty parsonage and throw frozen dinners into the microwave.

Jade swung back the door on the second ring. For the first time that morning, Tobin felt welcomed. Jade stood there, her effervescent smile stretching from ear to ear.

"Hey, Tobin, you're just in time to ride over to my folks' place with me."

"Then you have plans?"

"Doesn't everyone on Thanksgiving? My mother already has the turkey in the oven. I baked a couple of pies."

"Then I won't hold you up."

"What do you mean? Get in here. I'm not leaving for another twenty minutes. What about you?"

"I'm just having a lazy day."

As she reached the door to her bedroom, Jade spun around. "In other words, you're on your own?"

"The folks are gone and Jon had plans."

Jade's eyes clouded. "Woodward didn't tell you where he was going? What's the big secret?" she muttered sympathetically.

"I didn't ask. And Kedrick's off with Kip and Casey."

"Not good." Jade plopped down on the bed. "They're kind of rough-hewn. They belong to a rock band. When you cut hair, you meet a lot of people. Kedrick wants them at my birthday party."

"It's your party."

"I figured they'd see that painting in your living room."

Tobin did a double take. "The Emmaus Road?"

"It's very moving. So—are you going to dinner with me?"

"I'm not invited."

"I just invited you," she said with a merry chuckle. "Mom always has room for my brother's friends and mine. Besides, no one should spend the holiday alone. So that's settled."

"I'm not dressed."

Jade glanced at Tobin's blouse and slacks. "Nothing wrong with what you have on."

"Are you stopping by the nursing home to see Betts?"

Jade's gaze swept the room, her eyes tearing. "She's dead."

"Oh, Jade, I'm so sorry. Why didn't you call me?"

"I had to work it out myself. I was there three days ago. I was with her when she died. She just went to sleep. She's finally flying free." Her voice cracked. "It's what I always wanted for her. Betts had so many dreams before the accident. And nothing afterward."

"But you shouldn't keep your pain to yourself."

"I have my diary—I've kept one for years. It's filled with things about Betts and my ex."

"I haven't kept one since I was ten years old."

"You don't need to. You get your emotional work-out in the church. I keep my dreams and tears bottled up in my diary. Someday, maybe you'll get to read it." She smiled slyly. "Then your father will know how much I loved his God. And his deacons will know that I wasn't someone to fear because of my divorce."

"I don't think they feel that way."

"They do, but I don't blame it on you, Tobin." She wiped her eyes. "I keep my diary hidden because Kip comes around sometimes and I write about his visits. And Kedrick comes and I write about him. I like talking to Kedrick. I like trying to figure him out."

The words of the *SeaGull* captain came back to her. *That pretty blonde that I often see Jon with.* "Do you write about Jon Woodward?" she asked, plucking at a loose thread in the quilt.

"Mostly about you and Jon. And I write about my family because I love them so much. I want them to be proud of me."

"They are proud of you."

"I want them to be. But if anything ever happens

to me—like it did to Betts—then find my diary, Tobin, and throw it away.''

"That would be like tossing you out, Jade.''

"Then read it first before you throw it away. You'll
know me better if you do. Everything has a history,
a memory. I write everything down. You'll find that
out when the time comes.''

"You scare me when you talk like that.''

"Losing Betts and Cory has made me sad.''

They were sitting on the quilt Jade's grandmother
had made. She reached into a torn seam. "I keep the
diary here. You're the only one who knows that
now.''

It was a thick diary with a blue velvet cover. Jade
flipped it open at random and began to read out loud.

"My friend Beth died today. I cannot—must
not weep. She is flying free. I cannot think of
anything more beautiful than flying free. I wonder if she knows I sent her a dozen red roses?''

She turned back several pages and smiled at Tobin.
"I write about you sometimes, too. Listen.''

"Tobin Michelson has become my best friend.
But she has fallen in love with Jon Woodward.
He is easy to know. Easy to desire. I walked
along the beach at the wee hours thinking about
them. The surf was up and the wind flicked the
beach sand over my feet. Like Tobin I am full
of dreams and disappointments. I must not stand

in the way of my friends. I want them to be happy."

For a few minutes Jade read on. Poetic thoughts. Thoughts of dying and the great beyond. Glimmers of her search for God. A poem about the dusty road to Emmaus. Her fears about walking beside Christ without recognizing Him. There were heart cries about her past, and her obvious struggle at divorcing Cory.

"I thought Cory and I would go on forever. I keep slipping out of God's hand when things like that happen."

"You can't, Jade. Nothing can pluck you out of God's hand once you know Him."

Jade seemed surprised, relieved. "Then I'll write that in my diary tonight so I won't forget it."

She ran her hand over the soft velvet cover before hiding the diary between the folds of her quilt again. "Someday, Tobin, you can read the rest of it."

She rolled off the bed and began tossing her dirty clothes into a pillowcase. "I always do my laundry at the folks'."

In spite of the tears in her eyes, there was a fleeting, impish gaze, a quick chuckle. "Dad thinks I'm wearing out the washer. But I go out every week so they'll know how I am."

The mood swing was complete. Tobin couldn't read her expression. "Why would they worry about you, Jade?"

"Isn't that what folks are supposed to do, no matter how old we get? Promise me, Tobin, that when I fly free you will get my diary right away. You'll know when it's time for my parents to read it or whether you should throw it away.''

She shouldered her laundry bag and headed for the kitchen. Grabbing up her car keys and one pie, she headed for the door. ''Tobin, please get that other pie and let's get out of here.''

Jade's parents lived in a comfortable residential district, tucked away on a cul-de-sac with freshly mowed lawns and a colorful array of impatiens growing in the flower beds. Using her own key, Jade burst through the front door with a high-powered, cheery, ''Hi, everybody. I'm home. Brought a friend with me.''

Jade's mother met them in the hallway. She was a woman in her fifties and as fair as her daughter, with a creamy complexion, blue eyes and high cheekbones. She smiled. ''Dad and the boys are inspecting the workshop. They'll be in shortly.''

She hugged Jade, laundry bag and all, then leaned back and said, ''Jewel, how are you?''

Jade shrugged. ''I'm doing great. Really. Best grades ever.''

''You don't need money?''

''I told you I'm doing it on my own this time. I won't let you bail me out, not when I have clients all over the campus.'' She turned hurriedly. ''This is my friend Tobin. Her grandfather socked her with that name. By the way, she came for dinner.''

Helga Wellington took the announcement in stride and put another place setting on the decorative dining-room table.

"I'm embarrassed about barging in, Mrs. Wellington."

"No such thing. We have enough food for an army. Michael's and Jade's friends have always been welcomed in our home. So it's about time Jade brought you home so we could meet you. We've heard so many wonderful things about you."

"I even warned them you're a preacher's kid."

They could hear men's voices near the back porch; one of them sounded familiar. "Jade," her mother said, "Cory called."

Jade stiffened. "I'm not returning the call."

"He knows that. He just wanted to see how you were. To say hello to everyone. Honey, I told him about Betts." She wiped her hand on her apron. "He seemed genuinely sorry."

"He always is."

"You had another call, darling, from Dr. Harvey."

"The pediatrician? Mom, I'm almost twenty-four."

"But he's taken care of you all your life. He said it was time for a checkup. He won't renew your asthma prescriptions until you see him. Promise me—"

"I've got a rotten schedule, but I'll call him. Maybe I'll go during Christmas vacation."

"That's not soon enough."

"Don't worry, Mom. I haven't had a serious problem with my asthma for ages."

Tobin turned as three men came through the kitchen door. When she saw Jon she said, "I didn't know you would be here."

Helga said, "Oh, Mike and Jon have been friends for years."

Michael shook Tobin's hand. "I'm Mike, Jade's brother."

He was a commercial artist, a tall man with flaming red hair, long sideburns and blue eyes that danced when he smiled. He turned to the older man. "And this is Dad."

Tobin turned from Jon to face Paul Wellington, a stocky seagoing man with gray-blond hair. "Jade tells me you were a Coast Guard commander, sir."

"With the Coast Guard for over twenty years. And obviously, you've met Jon?"

"Yes, we've met." But we're strangers, she thought. No wonder he didn't tell me where he was spending Thanksgiving Day.

She glanced at Jade thinking, Did you deliberately bring me home for dinner so I would be embarrassed? So I would know that you had right of passage?

In the awkward silence that hovered around them, Jade said, "Mike brought Jon home years ago when they were in college."

Paul laughed. "And Jade took possession of him the day Jon walked in the door."

"She was ten," Helga said companionably as she lifted the turkey roaster from the oven.

Mike thumped Jon on the shoulder. "He's always been family to us, but for a while we thought Jade had her hooks in him. Even proposed to Jon when you were ten, didn't you?"

"That was the first time," she admitted.

Steam spiraled above the turkey. The aroma of Thanksgiving dinner filled the room. "Paul, carve the bird for us. And Mike, wake your wife and children for dinner."

"Come give me a hand, Jon," Mike said. "That

little Jennifer of mine is another blue-eyed angel with her eyes on you.''

He tweaked his sister's cheek as he left the room. ''Good to see you, Peewee. I miss you when you're not here.''

Jon looked helplessly at Jade and then at Tobin. ''I'm sorry, Tobby,'' he mouthed as he followed Mike from the room.

After dinner Tobin and the others gathered around Jon's chair to look at his latest snapshots of Angelo. He was a handsome child. Fringes of reddish-brown hair peeked out from his navy blue baseball cap. Beautiful wide brown eyes smiled back at her. He was wearing a white knit shirt with blue trim on the collar that matched the color of his cap. A row of brass buttons down the middle. In one picture Angelo's mouth was closed, his lips well formed. In the other his teeth were spaced and, like his ears, too big for his body. But he was small for his age; in time as he filled out and grew taller these would not matter. All anyone would see was the handsome child that Jon wanted for his own.

As Jade studied the pictures, Tobin saw again the deep compassion in her friend's expression. Through dinner, she had thought of Jade as competition, but now softened; she was certain that Jade had a heart that would welcome and engulf Angelo in a way that she might not be able to do.

Suddenly what would be right and best for Jon and Angelo was what mattered to Tobin. The tightness in her throat was unbearable, but she said, ''Jon, why didn't you bring Angelo to America for the holidays?''

His head tilted, his gaze meeting hers. "I told you, he doesn't have a British passport."

Helga laughed softly. "And, Jon darling, I rather imagine he doesn't have a passport from his own country."

"I want to adopt him," Jon said evenly, "but the courts are making it difficult. We're talking about a child without a country, without identity."

Paul pressed his fingers together. "And rightfully so that the courts go cautiously, Jon. You can't adopt a child whose parents might still be alive."

"And you're so unsettled, Jon," Helga told him. "Why, these months in Auburn are the first in years that you've been in any one place. That's no life for a child. You said he's happy where he is—that the woman who cares for him loves him."

"So do I, Helga. His present arrangement is only temporary. I've had more than one investigation going on—searching the area where I found him in Bosnia. Poring over the records that have been compiled. It's difficult, of course, without a name. But we have his description, his approximate age when I found him. But no one has listed a child like that as missing."

Kindly Jade said, "That could mean he has no one left."

"Or that someone thinks he's dead already," Mike added.

"The poor darling." Helga touched Jon's shoulder. "Why didn't you tell us what was going on? We knew—we knew about Jenna, but so little about this child. Why didn't you let Paul and me help you? We still can, if you need money."

Jon's gaze swept toward Jade, then back to her

mother. "You had burdens of your own. And if nothing came of the adoption, I didn't want anyone to know how much I cared for that boy."

One by one they took their seats again, leaving Jon sitting there with the pictures of Angelo in his hands. Jon looked stricken, weary. "I won't give up the fight to get him."

"But, Jon," Mike said, "if this child means so much to you, why didn't you stay there in the Cotswolds with him? The lawyers will notice your absence."

"Two reasons. First I would be tempted to take any photojournalism assignment that came my way. I would be gone and that would defeat the purpose. I was burned out. I had to get away."

"And your second reason?" Jade urged.

"We were getting attached. If adopting him fell through—" He cleared his throat, and this time he stared across at Tobin. "I wanted to break the tie now—to make it easier on him later. When this job at Auburn opened up I grabbed it."

"And what did you tell Angelo?" Mike's wife asked.

"That I loved him. That we'd always be friends. He knows I'm working here in America. I'm supporting him. He knows that, too."

Gently Helga asked, "Did you promise Angelo that you'd find a mother for him while you were in America?"

He looked at Tobin and Jade, and then glanced back to Helga. "No, Helga. I never thought I'd fall in love again."

Mike broke the growing tension, by grabbing for his camera. "I think we'd better get some holiday snapshots so Jon will have something to send back to Angelo.''

Within seconds he had them posing, and before the roll ran out he took several pictures of Jade and Tobin with Jon. ''I want the best smiles you can give me,'' Mike said. ''The three of you make a pretty good team.''

Jon slipped his arm around each girl. ''What a lucky man I am with my best friends beside me.''

Best friends. That was all Tobin could hope for. But at the moment it was important. She would go on with her plans for a birthday party for Jade and enlist Jon's help to bring it off.

A week later she received a copy of the snapshot in the mail. ''This one turned out best,'' Mike wrote on the back. ''Tobin, Jon, Jade. Best friends. Hang on to it for posterity.''

Tobin glanced at it and saw the beaming smiles on all three faces. She tacked it to her bulletin board, wondering what the future would hold, not knowing it was the last picture they would take together.

Chapter Thirteen

On the first Saturday in December Tobin walked briskly across the campus to the university's Olympic pool with the wind to her back and storm clouds threatening overhead. The gigantic pool was situated not far from the football stadium. The two buildings shared a choice piece of land that sloped gently in the east and still bore the name of the town's best-known philanthropist, Gilbert Gaspian.

A sunroof stretched the full length of the pool and the prefabricated sidings had been fitted snugly around the building to enclose the gym for the winter season. Tobin spotted her car in one of the spaces reserved for the press and gave it a quick once-over. No dents. Kedrick had delivered her vehicle without running amuck in the traffic. She used her spare key to put her briefcase into the trunk and grabbed her warmer coat.

Jon was waiting for her at the gate, waving two

tickets and showering her with that amiable grin of his. Unabashed, he leaned down and kissed her.

"Did you see Jade?" she asked, slipping her arm in his.

"Only a glimpse of her going in the side entry. She knows that we're getting together after the meet. And I saw Kedrick. You couldn't miss him squealing in on two wheels and slamming on the brakes. Why doesn't he use his own van?"

She hesitated, not wanting to tell him the truth. But Thanksgiving Day had opened up new vistas for them that included being honest with each other.

"Brent Carlson is on the alert for Kedrick's van."

"Another arrest?"

"Another warning. His last, according to Jade. I don't know how to help him, Jon. I'm frightened for him."

He wrapped his fingers around hers. "You enable him when you loan him your car."

She flushed at the rebuke. "Jon, he's my brother."

"All the more reason to keep him off the streets until he gets help."

"I think everyone is afraid of offending my family."

"Honey, you need to be more afraid that he will hit someone or hurt himself."

"I worry about that all the time." She rested her head against his shoulder. "I don't know how to stop him."

They were inside now, making their way to the third bleacher. Jon stepped back and let her take her seat ahead of him. Settled, with no air space between them, Tobin frowned; she glanced around, searching the press box for Kedrick. The stadium was filling quickly. It was one of those things she liked about Auburn—the way the people turned out for university functions. She waved at some friends and then looked back at the press box and then to the pool, anxious for the races to begin.

"What's wrong, Tobby?" Jon asked.

"I was looking for Kedrick. He's here somewhere."

"He's somewhere on the sidelines, waiting to snap pictures of Jade. I wish he didn't hang around her so much."

She gave him her attention. "Jon, you know he's the sports editor. It's his job to cover these sporting events."

He smiled patiently. "The ones he wants to attend? He likes Jade, but it can't go anywhere, Tobby. You of all people should know that—the son of Ross Michelson dating someone like Jade?"

She heard resentment in his voice and put her hand over his. "They're just friends, Jon. Jade wants to help him."

"Tell that to your brother. The next thing we know there will be a whistle-blower at the church making snide remarks about Jade. Some idiot who will make a scandal out of her past." She felt his hand flex. "Don't you understand, Tobin? Jade is vulnerable enough without being an outcast in the cathedral."

"Dad would never let that happen."

"Really? Maybe that was before his son started destroying them both. Honey, I expected problems with Kedrick's wild arrival here tonight, but he did seem clearheaded when I spoke to him.''

"See, I told you. Jade's good counsel is rubbing off.''

"Tobby, I don't want her hurt. Her ex left her emotionally drained. She doesn't need your brother making matters worse.''

She nodded, agreeing reluctantly. Was there any harm in their spending time together? She knew there was. Kedrick would never settle for friendship. And if Jade turned him away, what then? "Jade assured me she only wants to help him.''

"He needs a recovery program. Not Jade.''

She looked away, tears stinging her eyes. He touched her chin and turned her back to face him. "Jade means more to your brother than just a friend. You see that, don't you? He told me the other day that he'd like to put a ring on her finger for Christmas. He asked me to help him pick one out.''

A ring on her finger was what Tobin wanted for Christmas. But Jade and Kedrick? "Oh, Jon. Once she tells him no, I'm not sure what he will do.''

The spectators to Jon's right scowled at them as the first competitors lined up at the pool's edge. Jon winked at Tobin. "We'd better keep our eyes on the preliminary heats, Tobin, or we'll be taking some heat ourselves. We'll talk more later.''

"You think we're wrong to encourage Kedrick and Jade to go out with us after the meet?''

"At least we'll be there to support Jade,'' he said as he braced his foot against the bleacher in front of them.

Tobin shut out her clamoring heartbeat and turned her attention to the first eight competitors plunging into the pool and forming an uneven line as they slapped rhythmically against the water.

Finally, those competing in the preliminary heat for the breaststroke were announced. Jade appeared to stay focused as she led the others out from the dressing room, a rolled towel under her arm, goggles perched on top of her bright swim cap. She dropped her towel on the stool at the end of the pool, and kicked off her thongs. Wearing the colors of the university, she looked slim and confident in her form-fitting gold-and-sapphire swimsuit. She seemed to ignore the crowd in the bleachers as she stood at the end of the pool slapping her arms, wiggling her fingers, limbering up. Her mind, Tobin was certain, was bent on winning and qualifying for the winter finals.

There were three more main swimming events before the university closed down for the Christmas holidays. But knowing Jade, Tobin knew she would be back on campus daily, practicing her strokes in an empty pool with a security guard standing by.

If Jade recognized them she gave no indication. But Kedrick was standing nearby now, his camera lens focused on her. Jade gave him a hint of a smile, and then her full concentration was back on the task ahead. She adjusted her goggles as she waited for the referee's signal.

"Swimmers, step up," the referee called.

Eight swimmers stepped to the starting block.

"Go for it, Jade," Tobin whispered. "You can do it."

Jon beat the air with his fists. "And no false starts, Jade girl. We're counting on you winning."

The referee lifted the megaphone and bellowed, "Swimmers, take your mark."

Tobin watched Jade lean down above the glimmering water, her fingertips extended. Jade's bare feet balanced on the starting block, her red-polished toes curled on the edge.

The burping horn blasted.

Jade's poised body plunged into the water. They watched her break the surface ahead of the others— an exploding geyser as she moved her arms in a steady rhythm. The swimmer in the next lane chopped the water in a frantic effort to move ahead of Jade.

At fifty meters they flipped together, their feet shoving against the pool's edge. Jade churned the water effortlessly, her attention riveted on the finish line.

"Come on, Jade. Come on," Jon shouted.

Kedrick dashed along the pool's edge, snapping pictures as he ran. Now he was heading back in the same direction as Jade, almost slipping on the wet cement. He regained his balance as Jade's competition closed in.

Tobin saw Kedrick's lips move and knew he was shouting encouragement. It was impossible for Jade to hear him, but with a fresh surge of adrenaline, she stretched ahead of the others, her fingers grazing the wall seconds ahead of the girl in lane three.

Jade shook the water from her face and grinned triumphantly at the stands. The crowd in the bleachers sprang to their feet. Jon grabbed Tobin and hugged her. "She did it. She did it."

Jon was still savoring Jade's victory when they met her in the parking lot. "You did it and we're proud of you, Jade."

She flashed him her warmest smile. "Maybe I did it for you."

Kedrick stepped forward. "Forget Jon. I'm the one who's really proud of you."

Jade covered her mouth and coughed, a dry, irritating sound.

"Are you okay?" Tobin asked. "You're not getting a cold? The stadium was a bit chilly."

"I'm all right."

Jon reached out and pulled her coat collar tighter. "It's not your asthma?"

"Oh, Jon. You sound like my mother."

"Are your parents here?"

"They will be for tomorrow's race. Mom had to pick Dad up at the Coast Guard club this evening...and don't worry. I haven't had an asthma attack for ages."

"But you're restless and wheezing." He tousled her hair. "You're not overexerting yourself, kid?"

Jade smothered another cough and said, "Swimming is good for me. A good night's rest and I'll be ready for tomorrow's meet."

"Do you want to call dinner off?" Tobin asked.

"No, let's go. I don't want to change our plans."

Kedrick couldn't take his eyes from Jade. He was looking like his old self. Handsome. Charming—and possessive. With his eyes still on Jade, he said, "Tobby, let me take your car so Jade can ride with me."

Tobin saw the despair in Jade's expression. "No, Kedrick. I'll drive my own car."

"Wait a minute," Jon said. "You drive your car back to the parsonage, Tobin, and we'll follow in mine. Then the four of us can go out to dinner together."

"But I planned to take Jade home," Kedrick protested.

Jon ignored him. "Come along. Let's have a quick dinner. Jade has had a tiring day. I think we all have."

An hour later, after dropping off Kedrick's film at the *City Herald* and finding a nice quiet restaurant for a celebratory dinner, Jade still looked listless. The wheezing had eased, but Tobin was worried.

"Did you keep that appointment with your doctor?" she asked.

"No, and I must. My bronchial dilator is plumb empty."

"But you're racing again tomorrow, Jade."

"Well, I think my medicine is good for one more race. I left it in my locker at the gym." She smiled, appeasing their concern with an energetic burst of chatter and deciding that she wanted pie for dessert after all with ice cream dripping all over it. "After all, this is a celebration. A celebration of friendship."

It was eleven when they dropped Jade off at her apartment. Kedrick made an effort to get out of the car to see her to the door. She stopped him. "I know the way, Ked," she said kindly.

"Can I call you tomorrow?"

Tobin ached for him as Jade said, "I'm busy tomorrow with the swimming meet. Some other time, Ked."

He's not getting it, Tobin thought. He doesn't understand that she can only be his friend. But when he wakes up to that fact, what will happen to him? What will he do?

"Good night all," Jade said. "Thanks for sharing my victory with me. And, Jon, are you going to keep your promise to me tomorrow?"

Surprised, Tobin glanced at Jon's face shadowed in the darkness. His arm rested on the seat behind her, his fingers doing a drumbeat close to her ear. He seemed ready to renege, and then thought better of it. "All right, Jade, you won the race tonight, I'll keep my promise tomorrow."

"What promise?" Tobin asked as they drove away with Kedrick sitting sullenly in the back seat.

Jon cocked his head, his forced smile in the streetlight not overly enthusiastic. "You'll see in the morning. But somehow I think it will please you. It might even please your father."

"Are you coming to dinner?"

"I do like pot roast," he admitted. "Will Jade be there?"

"No," Kedrick snarled from the back seat. "She never eats a heavy meal before a meet."

On Sunday morning Jon Woodward slipped into the pew and sat down between Tobin and Jade. He didn't like it, but he was keeping his promise to Jade and determined to meet Ross Michelson's ground rules. He didn't have that many days before Christmas, and that was the day he planned to put a diamond ring in Tobin's stocking.

But if Tobin was surprised to see him, Ross Michelson looked even more startled. Michelson's expression went from surprise to displeasure, as though Professor Woodward were an unwelcome guest, as though Jon's very presence might upset the sanctity of the church that he pastored. But as Michelson read off the announcements, Jon decided he had misjudged the man. Something was troubling Tobin's father. He apologized to his congregation for starting the service late—good thing, since it got Jon there on time. Michelson's voice cracked as he apologized for being delayed by an emergency meeting with the elders, and for his failure as a pastor to live up to the requirements of a bishop.

None of it made sense to Jon, but he felt Tobin stiffen beside him. Something's brewing, he thought. He made some wild guesses. A scandal erupting in the church? An upheaval in the congregation that threatened Michelson's position? Whatever it was, he was certain that someone in the church had been singled out as the source of the problem.

That meant he was innocent. It was the first time he had darkened the door of the church. And problems in this sanctuary could hardly be blamed on K. T. Reynolds. Tobin's grandfather attended church only for weddings and funerals, and sometimes he missed those. Beside him to his right, Jade lowered her head and gazed down at the dark green hymnal in her hands.

Jade? Had Jade been singled out?

Jon mulled it over long into the sermon, and then his attention was drawn back to the earnestness in Michelson's deep voice. Michelson was talking about the Man called Jesus. About His trial. About Him being led to the judgment hall and falsely accused. He described the darkening of the sky when the Man died.

Jon's thoughts raced back and forth between England and Auburn. His mind filled with a little boy in England who was being tossed back and forth in the courts as he compared the injustice in England to that on the Galilean hillside. Jon rationalized the thinking of the courts in England and the crowd staring up at three crosses. As far as he could determine from the five-point sermon, the Man in the middle was an innocent victim.

A mistrial, Jon decided.

His thoughts strayed to the legal system that kept Angelo and him apart—an injustice that roiled inside Jon. He missed a part of the sermon, but caught the tail end about the centurion who recognized too late that Christ had been an innocent Man, a righteous Man. Jon figured that Pilate and the centurion had both blown it. For the first time in his life, Jon found himself admitting that he found no fault in the Man called Jesus.

Afterward, at the dinner table in the parsonage, Jon looked at Tobin's father. Ross Michelson was braced against the chair back, a proud, rigid man, sitting stiffly at the head of the table.

"I'm interested in that boy of yours in England," Ross said quietly. "Perhaps I can help."

"Don't get involved with my dad," Kedrick warned. "He'll have you swallowing up his doctrine. And after this morning it sounds like he's on the carpet himself. What's wrong, Dad?"

Gramps lifted his drooping eyelids. "So it's true," he said sleepily, "There are rumblings of discontent in the church. You're not going to take it sitting down, are you, Ross?"

Ross eyed his father-in-law. "Several of the elders want me to resign, effective before the New Year."

"Why, Ross?" his wife asked indignantly. "What have you done wrong?"

He met her gaze across the table. "I preach boring sermons."

"You can say that again, Dad."

"Kedrick," his mother cautioned.

Ross dabbed his lips with his napkin. "And I oppose letting the young people run with the crowd."

"Yeah, you're too vocal. No drinking. No divorce. No welcome mat to people like Kip and Casey because they look too rowdy."

"That's not true, Kedrick. Everyone is welcomed." Tobin looked desperately to Jon and back to her father. "I don't want my friends going away thinking the church has failed them. Everyone's welcomed. Right, Dad?"

"Not Casey and Kip," Kedrick said. "Not even Jade. Dad's got his own welcome list."

Mrs. Michelson bristled. "Stop it, Kedrick. You can gain nothing by dating a divorcée. Hear your father out."

"I want the young people to stand for something," Ross said.

"You've got to wake up, Dad, and go with the flow."

"Never, Kedrick," he said very quietly. "I'll resign first. I'll do what the elders want."

"Without a fight, sir?" Jon asked. "Sir, perhaps you are too troubled by the concerns of others."

"You're right, Mr. Woodward. But I'm more concerned about losing my son. His drinking is destroying all of us."

"Is that what your deacon board thinks?" Tobin asked.

"That and Kedrick's relationship with Miss Wellington."

Jon leaned forward. "There is no relationship between them, sir. Kedrick has to appreciate that Jade has no intention of marrying anyone again—for a long time."

"You're wrong, Jon."

"No, Kedrick," Tobin said. "You have to face the truth sooner or later. She's your friend. That's all."

His face contorted. "Tobby, I thought you were my friend. I thought you'd put in a good word for me."

"I can't work a miracle, Kedrick. You're sick. That's why Jade befriended you. Your drinking may cost Dad his job. But I think we love you enough to sacrifice anything for you."

"You need help, son. You have to get in a recovery program."

"I don't understand," his wife said. "There's nothing wrong with Kedrick. Why are you all picking on him?"

"Our son is an alcoholic. When will you admit it, Wini?"

Kedrick shoved back his chair and stomped from the room.

Tobin turned to her grandfather. "Say something, Gramps. This is getting out of hand."

K.T. sighed heavily. "I've been fighting my own battles with Ross here for more than thirty years. I didn't think I could do anything with him. But Ross is right. We've all been sitting back waiting for someone else to help Kedrick. This Jade Wellington is the first one wise enough to try."

He glanced at his granddaughter and put his burly hand on her arm. "Tobby, honey, don't go too harshly on your father. There are problems that we don't know about. And Kedrick—not your friends—may be the source."

He stood. "I have work at the paper. Come by any time, Jon. I'm just sorry that you had to be in on this family affair. But you've seen us at our worst—"

"And your best, sir."

Gramps and Tobin left the table together, arm in arm. To break the painful silence, Jon asked, "Why don't you and Mrs. Michelson go to the swim meet with us? You'd enjoy it."

Ross cleared his throat. "On Sunday?"

"Oh, let's do go," his wife begged. "This house

is like a tomb. I'm tired of playing the Sunday role. I want to be out there enjoying life.''

''All right,'' Ross said quietly. ''We'll all go. Leave the dishes, dear, and go change.''

Jon was left alone—sitting at the table with Ross Michelson.

''Well, Mr. Woodward, you have discovered that I am an imperfect man.''

''And for the first time, sir, I like you.''

Surprised, Ross asked, ''Was there something you wanted to talk to me about?''

''I've been meaning to talk to you about your daughter.''

Michelson's ashen face relaxed into a smile. ''I've been wondering when you'd get around to talking to me about Tobin.''

''You have been, sir?''

''You forget, Mr. Woodward, that I faced the same dilemma some years back. Thirty years ago, to be exact. That's when I had a talk with K. T. Reynolds about his daughter. And that, young man, was an extremely difficult challenge.''

Chapter Fourteen

December 11. Jade flipped the hangers across the narrow pole of her cramped closet, looking for just the right outfit for her birthday party. She paused, studying the old demure, cap-sleeved blouse for the third time and then, rejecting it again, kept on searching. This was a celebration—her twenty-fourth birthday. She should be bursting with joy, bubbling inside.

She was back in school with surprisingly good grades. Jon kept telling her that she was skillful with the camera and might find herself an opening in photography. He practically had a recommendation written out for her already. Her divorce had been final for months now. It was still a low point in her life, but these days she could think about Cory with a vague dismissal. But sometimes, like now, she hated being divorced. She had gone into marriage believing it to be a forever kind of thing.

Forever, she thought, had not lasted long at all.

She was back into her family's good graces. The

truth was they had always been there for her, proud
as peacocks that she was standing on her own. But
they fretted over her. Did she have enough money?
Was she eating right? Did she get enough sleep? Was
she taking her asthma medicine? Was she running
with the right friends? Yes, you couldn't lose with
Tobin and Jon. She knew what was behind her parents' concern. They were not blind. They had always
known that she had a crush on Jon, but hadn't realized
how important he was to her until Thanksgiving Day.

As they'd cleared the table that day, she had seen
tears in her mother's eyes and had known that she
understood. Forty-five minutes ago they had talked on
the phone.

"Mom, I'm thinking about transferring to another
college."

Her mother's gasp was audible. "And move away
from Auburn?"

"I won't go far. Maybe to Oregon or Arizona."

"Oh, darling, you'll lose your place on the swimming team."

She twisted a strand of hair. "I'll choose a school
that includes swimming in their sports program."

"It's Jon, isn't it?"

She worked the muscles in her jaw, forcing her lips
to move. "It hurts seeing Tobin and Jon together.
They're my best friends. I shouldn't be thinking about
Jon. Tobin is so right for him."

"Jade—you can't help your heart," her mother
said. "Jon will be gone by summer's end. Can't you
make it until then?"

"Betts didn't."

Betts! She didn't even have Betts to visit anymore. It had left a big empty hole inside, one that would have to heal from the inside out. "I miss those visits at the nursing home."

"I know, dear. Losing her at holiday time is just too much. Why don't you call off the birthday party and come home?"

"And disappoint Tobin? She still wants you and Dad to come to the party tonight. Can you?"

"No, we'd rather not. We plan to have a birthday dinner for you tomorrow. Roast turkey and dressing. Mashed spuds and gravy."

"My favorite. I think I'll pack my overnight case. Maybe even stay a few days. Is that okay?"

"Do you have to ask? Of course it's all right. We could take a drive up the coast."

"I'd like that. Carmel, maybe. I won't even have to think about Jon Woodward."

"Michael feels it's his fault—bringing Jon into our lives."

Jade laughed. "Mike always took the blame for everything. It'll work out, Mom. Part of it is my pride. As far back as I can remember, Jon was always there in my fantasy world."

"He's been a family fixture for years. Even when he was in Europe. Calling us the way he did. If your father and I had only known how you felt."

"You never guessed?"

"We passed it off as a childhood crush. Michael said to tell you someone special will come along for you someday."

"I hope I'm here when he comes...and not in

Oregon. I'd better get on with finding something to wear tonight. I'll see you in the morning. Love you."

Her mother was reluctant to let her go. "Jade— have you talked with Jon? Does he know how you feel?"

"I'm still a little kid to him."

"You're everything to your father and me. Your dad and I are both here for you. Always. I wasn't supposed to tell you yet, but Daddy is thinking about a long vacation this summer for the three of us. To Sweden and Norway. Our treat."

"So I won't be here when Jon and Tobin marry?"

"Wouldn't it be better if you were gone?"

"Tobin wants me to stand up for her."

"Doesn't she realize how much that would hurt you?"

"We've never discussed it."

"You're all right about the party? You know Jon will be there with Tobin."

"Yes, undoubtedly. They do everything together now."

"Don't take his class next semester. Avoid him."

"Bury my head like an ostrich? Mom, I've just switched to a communications major. I need his classes. Besides, Jon is one of my clients. I cut his hair every week."

Her mother's hearty chuckle rippled over the phone line. "No wonder he always looks so handsome."

Jade hung up feeling a snitch better. Business was down for the holidays, but the growth of her clip-and-style business kept her independent. And thanks to Tobin's grandfather—that lovable, affable grump—

she was getting good publicity on the *City Herald* sports page, even complimented for overcoming asthma and becoming a champion on the swim team.

Kedrick's photographs helped. They were some of his best work. With Kedrick's encouragement, even Tobin and Jon attended her swim meets. But it hurt to see them together when she climbed out of the pool.

She had barely gone back to preparing for the party when the phone rang again. "Jade, Jon here."

"Did Mother tell you to call?"

"She told me you were upset."

"Did she tell you to call?"

"No, just the opposite. She said to leave you alone. What have I done?"

"You moved to Auburn for a year. That was a big mistake."

"Are you all right?"

"Nothing's wrong. I'm just having birthday jitters trying to decide what to wear tonight so I'll look festive."

"You always look good."

"From a camera lens, Jon?"

"Jade, I'll see you at the party. And I hope you're in a better mood by then." He hesitated. "If you're sure everything's okay? Your mom sounded worried."

"She's worried about me since the day I was born. Mothers do that, you know. I'm on top of the world. But, Jon, we have to talk sometime."

She eased the receiver in place and went back to

the task of searching for an outfit. But her heart wasn't in it.

What's wrong? she mimicked. Everything.

In seven months she would be a senior at the university, have her old jalopy paid for and be completely out of debt. Her thoughts rarely stretched beyond that. She never pictured herself ten years from now, or twenty, or growing old. Mostly she thought about short-term events. The party. Tomorrow. Next week. But for the moment, with all that was going well, she felt ancient, as though all of life had passed her by: a ruined marriage behind her and a future that seemed unsettled—bleak without Jon in it.

Buck up, she told herself. It's your birthday! But still she felt down in the mouth—even the visits with Betts were no longer possible. She stared at the clothes on the rack again—the slinky black evening dress, the aqua suit that she'd worn Sunday, the wedge dress with its animal-print scarf. She wanted to wear something special—maybe a strapless party gown that would give the illusion of having stepped from a fashion show.

Or should she wear jeans and an oversize sweater as she was wearing now so that Kip and Casey would feel at home in the parsonage? She regretted asking them, knowing they would show up in baggy trousers and wild rock-and-roll T-shirts. They might feel like outcasts with the Michelsons' family Bible on the coffee table and the Emmaus Road on their living-room wall. She glanced down at the discarded outfits on the floor—worn jeans, slacks, blouses. And then, resolutely, she plucked a two-piece red dress from the closet and held it up to the light.

As she made her decision, the doorbell rang. She kicked the clothes pile out of her way and rushed to answer it. Kip or Casey? Or maybe Kedrick sulking at her door? But there was no need for any of them to drop by. She would see them at the party.

Holding the dress in her hand, she swung back the door and stared in surprise. "Oh, it's you."

Jon straightened his tie. "Obviously you were expecting someone else."

"I was getting ready for the party. I'm running short of time—I hope you don't need a haircut?"

"No, you did me two days ago. You said we had to talk."

"I didn't mean before the party."

"Jade, you sounded unhappy when I talked to you a half hour ago. What's up? You know I'm your friend."

She wanted him to be more, but she nodded and even managed a hint of a smile for him.

"May I come in?"

"Why not?" She drew back the door and held her breath as he strolled across to the sofa.

"Come here." He patted the spot beside him. "Let's talk."

She tossed the dress over the sofa back and faced him. "We only have a few minutes—the party, you know."

"They'll wait for you. You're the guest of honor."

"I don't feel much like partying."

"What's wrong, Jade? You sounded awful on the phone. That's why I came right over."

"You didn't have to."

"My choice. So what's up? Have I done something?"

You? Not you, she thought. I can only accuse you of stealing my heart a long time ago. But you don't know, do you? I'm just the little kid you watched grow up.

"I'm thinking about going away, transferring to a different school."

"But why? You've just gotten settled in here. You're doing so well with your courses, your business, the swim team." His bright hazel eyes held hers. "We're all proud of you. Whatever is troubling you, let it go."

Tears welled in her eyes. "Jon, I can't let something go that was never mine."

He frowned, the puzzle lines ridging his brow. "Jade, I've known you almost all your life. Surely you can trust me."

Perhaps she should tell him the truth. Clear the air. Make him understand why she had to go away. "You're thinking about getting married, aren't you?"

"Tobin and I are talking about it."

"That's why I must go away," she blurted. "I've been crazy about you all my life——but you're in love with my best friend."

If she had hit him, it could not have stunned him more. The muscles in his face twitched. "You? Me? Don't, Jade." He reached out and rubbed her wrist gently. "I'm not the one for you. I'm just a family friend. You were only a little kid when I met you."

"Nine or ten," she said. "I looked forward to those times when you would come home with my big brother."

He groped for words. "I used to roughhouse with you. You were a cute little kid."

"You even carried me on your shoulders once or twice down to the beach and dumped me in the ocean."

He laughed. "You deserved it. I dumped you in because you were pulling my hair. How old were you when I went away?"

"You left after my fourteenth birthday."

"I'd forgotten. You begged me to come to your party. You'd really grown up. I remember thinking how pretty you were all dolled up. You seemed so different without your ponytail."

"You took pictures of me that day."

"That's right. Your mom asked me to. I kept one of those pictures for myself. Even took it abroad with me."

"Why did you do that?"

"Because we were family and you were special."

But not special in the way that you have been to me, she thought. "I cried when you moved to Europe."

"I know. I still remember wiping the tears from your cheeks. I said, 'Look, little sis, I'll be back.'"

"I wasn't your little sis."

"But I've always thought of you that way. Still

do,'' he said firmly. ''That's why I'm here for you now. Kedrick isn't giving you a rough time, is he?''

''Kedrick Michelson? We're just friends. He needs friends. I know where he's coming from. Where he's heading if he doesn't get straightened out.''

''You've been like that all your life, haven't you, Jade? Always taking on somebody else's burden. Cory when you married him. Betts there in the nursing home. Kedrick—but I'm afraid he sees you as more than a friend.''

''He knows better. He had run out of friends when I came along. I run interference between Kedrick and his grandfather.''

''You're taking on the whole city newspaper.''

''No, just K. T. Reynolds. We've become friends since he's been publishing articles on me as Auburn's swimming champ. I keep telling K.T. that his grandson will come through someday. For now, I just want to be there for Kedrick so he won't fall apart.''

''Like you were there for me when Jenna died?''

''Oh that. All I did was write to you.''

''It meant a lot to me. And you wrote when you heard about Angelo.''

''I guess I just like to write letters.''

''I never read between the lines. Will you forgive me, Jade?''

''For what, Jon? For not knowing how much I cared about you? Didn't you even guess? Ever?''

''Since coming to Auburn, the thought passed through my mind. But I brushed it aside. I would never hurt you, Jade.''

''You did it without even trying. Tobin talks about

you all the time and I have to pretend that you are just my brother's friend. We even joked about all the girls on campus who knew you were single and available. I told her I was in competition with her and she just thought I was teasing.''

"You make me sound like I'm a prize in some contest.''

"Tobin is a wonderful girl, Jon. You know that, don't you?''

He nodded, his hand still resting on her wrist.

"Now you know why I'm thinking about going away. Tobin is my best friend.''

"Mine, too,'' he said. He glanced at his watch. "Right now she probably wonders where we are. I promised her I'd help decorate for your party and hang some streamers from the chandelier.''

"I promised to go early to make sandwiches.''

He stood. "Would you like to ride over with me?''

"No, I'll take my own car.''

"Then I'll head home and change.'' He towered above her, his gaze sympathetic. "Can we still be friends, Jade?''

She fingered her locket. "No need to change that, is there?''

He leaned down and kissed the top of her head as he had done when she was a little girl standing on tiptoe, begging him to take her with him. He started to walk away, then said, "Promise me, Jade, you won't quit school. You've come too far to quit now. You can't leave Auburn. You've been happy here.''

"Staying here would always remind me of you.''

The ringing of the telephone cut off his answer.

"Hello?" She cupped her hand around the mouth-piece, feeling troubled. "Of course I'm going to the party.... No, I don't have time right now. Oh, all right. At the Knightbridge Café.... Don't take another drink. I'll be there as soon as I can.... Yes, I'll hurry. I should be there in thirty minutes.

"You crazy idiot," she muttered as she severed the call.

"Is everything all right?" Jon asked.

"Of course," she wheezed. "Why shouldn't it be? It's my twenty-fourth birthday. I have nothing new to wear. I have to run an errand on the way to the party—and I just bared my heart to my best friend's fiancé."

He listened intently. "You're wheezing. Are you all right?"

"Stop asking me that. I've had a lot going lately. And Betts's death on top of it."

"Let's call the party off. Tobin would understand."

"Tobin would be disappointed." Without thinking, Jade tugged at her necklace. The chain snapped and tore free from her neck. She looked at the diamond-studded emerald in her hand and burst into tears. "And now this. I was going to wear it this evening."

He was back at her side at once, wiping the tears from her cheek as he had done when she was four-teen.

"My grandmother gave me this on my fourteenth birthday."

"I remember. I saw her take it off and give it to you."

"Because I was crying...because you were going away."

"Give it to me, Jade. I'll have it repaired for you."

She dropped it into his hand and wrapped his broad fingers around it. "I don't think I'll need it again. Would you—would you give it to Tobin someday?"

"To Tobin? Your grandmother's necklace?"

"Give it to her as a wedding jewel. You know, the bride always wears something new, something borrowed, something blue."

He looked down at the glimmering jewel in his hand, smiling faintly. "The emerald is green."

"But it is very old. And Tobin has always admired it. Will you give it to her? I want her to have it."

Now he looked worried, his smile gone. "Why not give it to her yourself?"

"I might not be around when you get married."

Chapter Fifteen

Tobin stood in the middle of the kitchen, her hands on her hips, an apron around her waist. She ran a mental checklist. The sandwiches were made, the platters of cookies set out on the table. The coffee-maker was ready to plug in. The crystal punch bowl only needed the ice cream at the last minute. The party napkins with teacups on them were folded. The house was spruced up.

Still she felt muddled trying to pull it all together. She wanted it to be perfect for Jade, but throwing a party was harder than writing a thesis. How could she blend thirty or forty personalities as different as Kip and Biddy from Jon's boardinghouse? As different as Casey who loved rock and roll and the quiet church organist who had befriended Jade?

Jade, she decided, had a conglomeration of friends. The bank teller from town. Wally the quarterback. The aides from the nursing home. Classmates and childhood friends. Her spunky ski instructor. Members of the swimming team. The seventeen-year-old girl next door who always felt left out. The grocery clerk. Her high school English teacher. People that Jade had befriended. People who laughed when they were with her. People who made her laugh. And Gramps. Gramps would be the only oldster at the party.

Everybody seemed to like Jade, and this pleased Tobin.

But yesterday Tobin had panicked. She hadn't planned out the evening. Other than the video that Jon had put together on Jade's twenty-four years, nothing else was organized.

"Everything will be fine," Jon had reassured her when he'd called. "I'll be there two hours ahead of time to help out."

"Then you can hang the streamers and put the chairs around the living room."

"As good as done."

"I need more party hats."

"I'll pick some up when I buy the film."

"You'll set the video up for me, Jon?"

"Nothing to set up. We'll just pop it in the VCR."

Kedrick had promised to pick up the cake. And while she mused over them both being late, she heard Kedrick bang out of his basement apartment and roar off in the van.

"Kedrick, where are you going?" she asked aloud. "You don't even know what bakery to go to."

"Hi."

She turned around, surprised to see Kip standing in the doorway. "I didn't hear the doorbell, Kip."

"Your folks let us in on their way out. Your dad told Casey to put the chairs up." He grinned sheepishly. "I think he's sloughing off on the job. That's him playing the piano."

She listened to a classical number as someone's fingers moved skillfully over the keys. "I thought he played the drums."

"He does." Kip pushed his long hair back from his face and secured it with a rubber band. "He grew up on the piano."

She had pushed Kip and Casey into a rock world of their own, one apart from hers. Snubbing them because they were different.

"We came early to help out. Jade is pretty special, you know."

"To all of us. Does Casey play the birthday song?"

"He plays everything by ear." As she glanced at the wall phone, he said, "You look upset, Tobin."

"I am. Jon—Professor Woodward—was supposed to be here early to hang some birthday streamers for me."

"I'll hang 'em. Tell me where."

She saw for the first time that he had a boyish face, a friendly smile. He wore a plain white T-shirt this time and faded jeans. "We put our present in the living room," he said. "We wrapped it in newspaper. Have to live up to our image, you know."

Suddenly she liked him. She led him into the large dining room and saw his eyes widen with pleasure at the well-laid table.

"The streamers are there on the cadenza, Kip."

"Right on. Any other jobs? Casey's got two hands, too."

"Kedrick was supposed to pick up the birthday cake."

"We kind of figured you might need us. We almost swallowed our teeth when the reverend opened the door. But he was right polite to us. Told us to have a good time." He turned toward the living room where another song filled the air. Strauss this time. "Cut the concert, Casey," he called. "We've got work to do."

Back at the apartment, Jade was heading toward the door when she ran back into the bedroom and tossed her shoulder bag on top of the quilt. There was a distinctive thud as it hit her diary. Turning to the wall opposite her bed, she studied the picture hanging there—the California coast with the Pacific raging in and washing over the weather-beaten rocks. She had loved it when she bought it. Still did. But lately the churning waves constantly reminded her of her past. She was looking for a future. A quiet, peaceful one.

Someday she would pass the picture on to Kedrick. He loved the ocean, surfed there often, his moods as changing as the sea. She hoisted the painting from the hook and shoved it end-to-end into her closet. Returning to the middle of her room, she noticed the faded spot where the painting had been and hoped that her birthday gift from Tobin would be large enough to cover it. She envisioned an Emmaus Road painting of her own hanging there—of awakening to its brilliant colors in the morning and contemplating its meaning.

If Reverend Michelson kept his word, he would have put a bug in Tobin's ear and Jade would not be disappointed. This evening in the midst of cake and ice cream she would unwrap her presents. She knew there would be some. She loved giving gifts herself, and thrilled at the expectation of unwrapping her own and finding a copy of the painting among them.

But there was one present she dreaded—a piece of fine jewelry or a ring or something equally personal from Kedrick. He was getting too involved, wanting to consume her time, then drowning himself into a stupor when she refused to see him. What had started out as her deep concern for a young man in need had become a nightmare. He was Tobin's twin. Marvelously handsome. Even more charming than Jon. But he was, as she warned herself again, too much like Cory. Desperately unhappy. Out of control. Too angry with his father. And clinging to his twin sister, holding Tobin back from her own happiness. Jade dared not come between them.

The phone rang, but she ignored it. Whoever was calling would undoubtedly be at the party. She brushed some dust from the wall, tugged at the hook to check its strength. Satisfied, she reached her hand into the seam of her quilt, rescued her diary and began to write.

> I will be home late this evening. Tired no doubt and too exhausted from the excitement to write in my diary. So I write now even though someone is waiting for me at Knightbridge's. I worry about seeing him, and yet, it is time to tell

him that we will never be more than friends and if he persists, even our friendship will shatter. He needs me because I understand him.

Oddly enough, I feel more at peace now contemplating the painting of the Emmaus Road on my wall, the comfort of it. It was good to talk to Mummy this evening, to hear her reassuring voice. To sense her love. I will toss my things in my overnight case first thing in the morning and be on my way. It will be splendid to have a birthday dinner with the family and then ride up the coast with Mom and Dad, just the three of us. My family is so special to me. I'm glad they know about Jon. I'm glad that they know that Jon and Tobin are my best friends; they are so right for each other.

She hesitated, her pen poised, and then she finished jotting her thoughts in her diary and hid it once more in the quilt that her grandmother had made. She ran her fingers over the top, soft as her grandmother's skin had been—an old-fashioned quilt stitched together with her grandmother's love.

Reluctantly she picked up her purse, glanced around the little room she loved, then left. She found a cramped parking spot a block from Knightbridge's and ran to the café, bursting into a crowded room smelling of fish and chips and ringing with blaring music. She hurried to Kedrick's table and slipped into the bench across from him before he could stand to welcome her.

"You're late," he complained.

"And you're making me even later for my own party." She was relieved to find him sober. He was drinking, but it was coffee. She moved her hand so the waitress could pour her a cup. "What was so important that you had to see me right away, Kedrick?"

"I wanted to give you something, Jade."

As the waitress walked away he reached into his jacket pocket, pulled out a jewel box and snapped it open. "I planned to give this to you for Christmas, but it's your birthday—"

"Don't. I can't accept that."

"But I thought…"

Jade stared at the solitary diamond. "I don't know what you thought, but no rings. We're friends. Just friends."

"Jade, you must know how I feel about you."

She shook her head. "I never led you on."

He glared at the box on the table. "I need you, Jade."

"I'm not the answer to your problems."

"I don't have a problem."

"Then why do you drink?"

"So I can sleep nights."

That brief measure of peace that she had sensed as she left the apartment plummeted. She felt a terrible tightening in her chest, that feeling that her lungs were whistling. She rummaged in her purse. Searched it again. Where had she put the bronchial dilator? She vaguely remembered putting it on her washstand. It was too late to go back to the apartment. She would have to make it through the party without it.

"Are you all right?" he asked.

All right? You make me totally stressed out and you ask me that? She said, "I'm fine. I have to get to the party. You're coming, aren't you?"

"I don't think so."

She knew he had to or he would end up drowning his sorrow. He wouldn't be fit to drive. "You can't disappoint Tobin."

"She'll get over it."

He wrapped his hand around the velvet box and dropped it back into his pocket. "I wanted us to go to the party together. I wanted you there as my girl."

"I'm sorry, Kedrick."

Her mood was hitting rock bottom, matching his. How could she even pretend to be festive when she reached the parsonage? What excuse would she give if Kedrick didn't show up?

"I want you there, Kedrick. Please go for my sake?"

She began to cough, that horrible racking cough.

Alarmed, he said, "You look like the pits."

"I feel like it," she admitted.

"Because of me?"

"Because of so many things. I wanted this evening to be perfect and now I'm down in the dumps. I'll end up making everyone miserable."

"Do you want something?"

"What do you mean?" She stared at him with a puzzled frown.

"To pep you up, I mean. Some pills. Over-the-counter stuff. Truck drivers use them to stay awake. I have some, if you want to try them."

She recoiled. No wonder his life was coming apart.

"No," she said. "You know I don't take anything like that."

"It's just something over-the-counter. No big deal."

She put her purse strap over her shoulder. "I have to go."

"You didn't drink your coffee."

"I'll grab one to go on my way out."

For a moment he looked congenial, concerned, his handsome face innocent. The teal of his sweater matched the color of his eyes and she thought again what a handsome pair the twins were.

"Give me a second, Jade. I'll get the coffee for you."

He returned with a medium-sized paper cup, hot to touch and smelling of cappuccino. "Happy birthday, Jade. Don't tell sis you saw me. But I'll try and drop by before the party's over."

Jade left, certain that his sullen gaze followed her to the door. She tried to relax as she drove to the parsonage sipping coffee. She felt as if she was breathing through a straw, as though her throat had shut off with every swallow. She pulled into the Michelson driveway, parked her car beside Tobin's and put on a cheerful smile as she rang the bell.

Tobin looked harried, an apron around her waist. "I thought you would never get here."

"I'm late. I'm sorry."

"Jon isn't here either. He was due an hour ago. And Kedrick drove off in that old van of his. It will be a miracle if he even remembers the party. But Kip and Casey are here—and they've been lifesavers." She pulled Jade into the entryway and gave her a quick hug. "Happy birthday, old thing."

"Twenty-four. Would you believe it?"

"Better than almost twenty-seven. You look lovely in that dress. Red is a good color for you." She made Jade whirl around. "But something is missing."

Jade's hand went to her breast. "My necklace."

"That's it. No emerald tonight?"

"The chain broke this evening."

"It didn't? Is that why you didn't answer the phone? I thought you'd never show up, so I called. But Kip and Casey came early. They put the decorations up for me and went after the cake. The cake's in the middle of the dining-room table."

"Oh, I want to see it—"

"Not on your life. Not until later. I had trouble enough keeping Casey and Kip from licking the icing. And you have a sweet tooth."

"At least tell me what it says."

Tobin was as excited as Jade. She disliked holding back surprises. "Well, it has this cute little girl in a swimsuit with scissors and clippers in her hand. And in pink and yellow icing it says, 'Happy Birthday to a Jewel of a Friend.'"

Jade wheezed as she said, "I'll never understand why you have been so good to me, Tobby."

"How could I help it when you're so good to everyone?" A frown furrowed Tobin's brow as she led Jade into the kitchen. "Are you having trouble breathing, Jade?"

"Just a little. My chest is tight. I feel like I'm being smothered with a blanket just trying to get my air."

"Not another bout with asthma?"

"Oh, no. I just wore myself out hurrying."

Tobin glanced at her watch. "The guests won't start arriving for another thirty minutes. And thanks to Kip and Casey, I have everything under control. Why don't you go lie down and rest?''

"You wouldn't mind?''

"Of course not. You know your way to my room.''

Jade held up her half-empty cup. "I don't want the rest of this coffee. It has a wretched flavor, anyway.''

"I'll take it. So scoot. We'll party in thirty minutes.''

At seven-thirty Tobin swung back the front door. Jon and the winter wind swept in. She had planned a lecture, at least a gentle scold for coming late. The look of contrition on his face and the unblinking gaze piercing hers changed her mind.

He thrust a mixed bouquet into her hand.

"Oh, for Jade. How sweet of you, Jon.''

"No, for you, Tobby. I'm really sorry I didn't get here earlier. Just show me what you want me to do.''

"I had other help,'' she said coyly. "Members of the rock band are here.'' She half closed the door as she sniffed the flowers. "Kip and Casey have the place all decorated. A bit more gaudy than I planned, but it's festive. Jade will like it.''

"I wasn't sure those two would come. I didn't want them feeling like fish out of water.''

"It's the rest of us swimming on dry land, Jon.''

He frowned. "I lost you.''

She cupped his cheek with her free hand. "I took a good long look at me this evening and I didn't like what I saw. I mouth off a lot about the Shepherd. But tonight, watching Kip and Casey doing things for Jade, I got a glimpse of the Shepherd's compassion. No wonder God brought Jade into my life. She is so caring. No wonder her friends adore her. I needed a friend like that.''

"So do I," Jon said. "What's that old saying about a friend sticking closer than a brother?''

"That's straight from the Good Book, Jon.''

"You're kidding!''

"I don't joke about some things.'' She smiled. "What are we standing in the entryway for? Half of the guests are already here. Casey's entertaining then. That's Casey on the piano.''

"Sounds good.''

"Sounds Gershwin. I wish Dad could see that side of him. Come on. Get away from the door so I can shut it completely.''

He didn't budge.

"What's wrong with you? Move. I'm cold just standing here.''

He leaned around the casing and grabbed a large gift from the porch. "I almost forgot to pick up Jade's birthday present.''

"Thank goodness you remembered.''

He looked sheepish. "The truth is the store manager called and reminded me. He held the store open until I got there. Biddy at the boardinghouse wrapped it for us.''

"Was the framing all right?''

"They did a great job. Jade will love it.''

Tobin reached up on tiptoe and kissed him. "I can hardly wait for her to see it. She's wanted that painting a long time.''

"It will overshadow everything else in her tiny apartment.''

"How do you know it's too big, Jon?''

"Her brother and I helped her move in.'' More

seriously, he said, "Tobby, when I realized I had forgotten to pick up the painting, I figured you'd put me
out to pasture. I'd be walking my own lonely Emmaus
Road."

"Like Jade has been doing?"

"Like we all do sometime in our life. That picture
really gets to you, Tobby. The artist did a great job."

Tobin bit her lower lip. "You know, don't you?
Jesus is the focal point of that painting. That's why
people are drawn to it."

"No sermons," he reminded her, slipping out of
his raincoat and hanging it in the hall closet.

"Just leave our gift by the door. Kip volunteered
to welcome the guests and arrange the gifts. You did
bring the video?"

As he patted the bulging pocket of his tweed jacket,
she realized again how striking he was—a charming,
well-groomed man with tantalizing aftershave. He
towered above her, those deep-set eyes dancing and
twinkling as he looked down at her. She took his hand
and led him into the kitchen, knowing they would not
be alone for long. But later, maybe by midnight, they
could spend a few moments together. Just the two of
them.

When they reached the kitchen he untied her apron
and tossed it aside. She turned to face him, laughing
up at him. Unmindful of the guest in the doorway, he
took Tobin in his arms and kissed her soundly. After
a breathless moment, she pushed him away and
brushed back her hair.

"I like it when you blush like that, Tobby."

Down the hall they heard the excited mumble of
more guests arriving. "Jon, I'd better get the ice
cream in the punch bowl and plug in the coffeepot."

He reached behind him, his eyes still on her, and plugged the cord into the outlet.

"The ice cream," she said as he reached out for her again.

He blew on her ear. "Let the members of the rock band take care of that."

"Already done," Kip said, brushing past them with empty ice cream cartons in his hands. "Don't mind me. But somebody better rally the guest of honor."

"Oh!" Tobin exclaimed. "Jade."

"She's already here?" Jon asked.

"She's in my bedroom resting. With everyone arriving I'd better go awaken Jade and let her freshen up for her guests."

Tobin ran up the stairs toward her bedroom, singing, "Happy birthday to you. Happy birthday…"

She shoved back the door and turned on the switch, flooding the frilly, pink room with light. Jade moaned on the bed.

"Get up, sleepyhead. It's party time."

Tobin was laughing as she crossed the room to the bed and then she was screaming.

Chapter Sixteen

Tobin stood frozen, unable to move, as Jon knelt by the bedside and took Jade's limp hand. Jade's lungs wheezed and whistled as she struggled to breathe.

"Tobin, call 911," Jon demanded.

"I already did," Kip said.

Jon turned with a vengeance on the guests crowding in the doorway behind him. "Kip, get them out of here."

"You heard the professor. Move. Get out. Jade will be okay. Professor Woodward has everything under control."

They backed away without a word.

"Jon, is it her asthma?" Tobin cried.

He put his mouth to Jade's and attempted to blow a few puffs of air into her lungs. "It's no good." He tossed Jade's purse to Tobin. "Check her purse. Look for her medicine."

Tobin dumped the contents on the dresser, her

hands shaking as she spread them out. "Her medicine isn't here."

"It wouldn't do any good anyway," he said hopelessly. "She would have to use it herself."

They heard the sirens approaching, the emergency vehicles roaring down the street. They screeched to a stop in front of the parsonage, lights flashing. The paramedics barged into the room, Brent Carlson and another police officer right behind them.

"What do we have here?" the paramedic asked.

"An asthmatic," Jon told him.

"Name?"

"Jade Wellington."

He slapped her face, trying for a response. "Jade. How you doing? Looks like a party going on. Been drinking? Taking drugs?"

"She doesn't drink," Jon said angrily. "Nor do drugs."

They were fast, efficient. Checking Jade's vital signs. Placing her on a hard board. As one hung an IV, another man inserted a breathing tube to ease the flow of air in and out of her lungs.

Jade struggled against their efforts, but her eyes were still closed. She was far from awareness. The paramedics looked to John for answers. Address? Allergies? Medications? Insurance?

"Cut the questions and get her to the hospital."

"She's young."

"Twenty-four today. We were celebrating—"

"You a relative, Mr.—?"

"Jon Woodward. A close family friend."

As the paramedics worked feverishly, Brent Carlson prowled around the room, his eyes finally settling on Jade's purse.

"What are you doing here?" Tobin asked him.

"I heard the emergency call on my frequency. We always try to show up in case we're needed. I was close by."

"Close by? What for? Were you looking for Kedrick?"

"Not this time. I was in the neighborhood anyway, what with all the cars parked on the street. I just wanted to know everything was all right. What were you celebrating?"

"Jade's birthday."

"That's a tough one. Sorry. She looks familiar."

"She's on the university swim team."

"No wonder I recognized her."

As they placed Jade on a stretcher and rushed her toward the door, Jon squeezed Tobin's hand. "Honey, you go to the hospital with them. I'll drive over and get the Wellingtons."

"You can call them from here," Brent suggested.

"This isn't something you shout over the telephone wires, Carlson. I'd rather tell them in person."

"Then I'll take Tobin to the hospital in the squad car. Bring Miss Wellington's purse. We may need it."

She nodded. Her bedroom was in shambles. The bedspread askew. The pillow wet where Jade's head had lain. The chair pushed aside where the stretcher had been. She ran her hand over the bedside table and swept the tissue into the wastebasket, her fingers catching on a key chain. Jade's keys.

She turned off the bedside lamp, wrapped her fingers around Jade's keys and slipped them into her pocket. Brent followed her through the house to the kitchen as she turned out the lights.

Kip stood in the doorway again. "I've told everyone to go home. But I think they're heading to the hospital."

"All this food," Tobin said aimlessly.

"I'll put it away."

"Oh, Kip, you are so good—"

"That's not how people usually describe me."

She rubbed the lump in her throat. "They don't know you."

Brent grabbed a sandwich as he unplugged the coffeepot, his eyes traversing the kitchen. "Have everyone leave their name and phone number, Kip. In case we have to get in touch."

He turned to Tobin. "Where's Kedrick?"

"How would I know?"

"He's your brother. He lives here." He ran his hand over the countertop. "Someone's been to Knightbridge's," he said, picking up the half-empty paper cup from the sink.

Absently Tobin said, "Yes, Jade had coffee on her way here. She said it tasted terrible."

He gave her a hard look as he opened the container. "It smells like coffee." He put his finger in and tasted it. "Odd taste. Do you have a plastic bag? I'll just take this along."

"Just have a fresh cup," she offered.

"This one will do. Something set Miss Wellington's asthma off. This, maybe. What about food? Did she eat anything?"

"She didn't say. Let's go, Brent."

Still he lingered. He glanced at the flowers in the vase and sniffed those, too. "Does she have trouble with flowers?"

"With ragweed and gardenias. I don't know what else. I just don't know, Brent. Stop asking me impossible questions. Just get me to the hospital. My friend is ill."

"Sorry, Tobby. I was hoping your brother would come home." He touched her elbow and led her outside. As they drove along with the lights flashing, he radioed in. He gave the description of Kedrick's van and his license number. "If you spot it cruising around town, pick Kedrick Michelson up and take him to the hospital. Yeah, Auburn General."

"What's that about, Brent? Kedrick hasn't done anything."

"I'm just trying to help your brother. He attends Wellington's competitions. I've seen him there. But not her party? Shouldn't he know that something's happened to her?"

At the hospital Brent stirred through Jade's purse again and found a small notebook with five phone numbers in it. "Mrs. Wellington," he asked, "are these numbers familiar to you?"

Helga Wellington stared blankly at the numbers with red-rimmed eyes. "My daughter is a hairstylist. They may be clients. Why are you here asking me these things at a time like this?"

"Just to be helpful, ma'am." He put the notebook

back into Jade's purse and handed it to her. "We'll keep in touch."

Tobin pulled him aside. "What did you do with the coffee?"

"I turned it over to the emergency room. The doctors think she may have ingested some drug and had a massive reaction to it."

Tobin gasped. "She only takes medication for her asthma."

"Then we have nothing to worry about."

"Brent, right now you are making me very angry. Jade didn't take things. Whoever gave her something—"

"Tobby, whatever it was, she may have taken it herself."

"No, Brent. She wouldn't do that."

Forty-eight hours later, as Jade slipped deeper into a coma, more friends filled the hospital lobby, refusing to vacate the premises as long as she was ill. When Jon spotted Kedrick among them, he turned to Mike Wellington. "That's the *Herald*'s sports editor over there, Mike. Kedrick Michelson—the one who has a serious crush on Jade. Brent Carlson brought him in."

"Was Michelson the one with her at the café?"

"Everyone is tight-lipped. But he hung around her a lot."

They confronted Kedrick together. "I want you to go into the unit with me and see my sister," Mike said.

Kedrick reared back. "It's against the rules."

Mike's jaw stiffened. "Our family is setting the rules."

Kedrick held his ground, staring angrily up at Mike and then at Jon. "No, I am not going in there."

"Oh, but you are. You're going in there if we have to drag you every step of the way. You're one of my sister's friends. Did you know a friend of hers met with her before the party?"

"I don't know anything about it, Mike."

Moments later as the three of them framed the curtained cubicle, Kedrick's eyes roamed wildly over the hissing equipment. Mike gave him a shove. "Go on, Kedrick. All the way in."

At the bedside he gripped the rail and closed his eyes.

"Open your eyes, Michelson," Jon told him. "You can't say goodbye with your eyes closed."

Kedrick's eyes opened slowly, the usual wide innocent gaze gone. He focused on Jade's face. As he stared down at her, he mumbled over and over, "I'm sorry, Jade. I'm sorry."

"Someone put something in Jade's coffee, Kedrick. One way or the other Mike is going to find that person and tear him limb from limb."

Kedrick shuddered. "We were friends. You know that, Jon. Ask Tobin. I wouldn't do anything to hurt Jade."

"We didn't ask you that. We just want to know if you saw Jade two nights ago, just before the party."

He was sweating profusely. "No. Now let me out of here."

* * *

On the fourth day as Jade's condition worsened, Tobin slipped beyond the forbidden door and stepped into the Intensive Care Unit. She stopped at the sucking sound of the respirator. Voices on the overhead swirled around her. She made her way to the second cubicle. Jade lay there in a blue hospital gown, motionless where they had placed her. She was all tubes. Tobin tried to focus past the machinery and the technical world that Jade had so despised. Behind it all, Tobin saw Jade's shiny blond hair flowing over the pillow, her body as still as death itself.

A nurse gripped Tobin's arm. "I'm sorry, but you really must leave. We've told you and your friends. Only family members can visit in the ICU."

"She stays," Helga Wellington said. "She's my daughter's best friend. She stays."

Her face was as white as the bed linens. "You can come any time, dear. Any time," she repeated for the nurse's benefit.

"Oh, Mrs. Wellington, if I had only found Jade sooner."

Helga touched Tobin's cheek. "No, dear Tobin, what happened was not your fault." She seemed to find a strength deep within her to say, "We talked to the doctors again an hour ago. The tests are back. There was a medication in her coffee—something fairly common they say that wouldn't normally be harmful, but Jade's asthma triggered an allergic reaction."

Tobin recoiled. "Jade always took her coffee black."

"We can't convince the doctors, but Paul and I

know—no matter what the doctors think or say—our daughter did not take something deliberately.''

"We looked for her inhaler, Mrs. Wellington."

"We know. Poor Jade. She was getting careless about carrying it. She felt like she was so much better."

"She'll get better again, Mrs. Wellington. You'll see."

"The doctors don't think so. Nothing would have stopped what happened." Her teeth chattered as she said, "It was a respiratory allergy, but she went into cardiac failure in the ambulance. Again in the emergency room."

"But she'll get better. You don't die from asthma."

Mrs. Wellington's shoulders convulsed. "It happens sometimes. We never thought it would happen to Jade."

They linked arms and found the courage to walk to the bed. Jade looked peaceful, untroubled, her brilliant blue eyes closed, her body trapped by machinery. The sheet was folded back over her feet, leaving the pink polished toes exposed. Her father hung over the side rail, holding her hand, saying his own goodbye. The clock beneath the monitor raced almost as fast as Jade's heartbeat.

Remembering her visit to Betts's bedside, she stroked her friend's brow and said, "Hi, Jade. It's your friend Tobin. I'm here with you. Jon is out in the lobby. He sent his love."

The only answer was the gushing of Jade's life support, the beep of her monitor. Tobin leaned over the side rail and gently clasped Jade's hand. "You've got to hurry and get well. You promised me you'd stand up for me when Jon and I get married."

Beep. Beep. Beep.

"A wedding?" Mr. Wellington shook his head. "Surely Helga told you. The doctors don't expect Jade to make it through the night." He flicked his hand toward the dreaded respirator. "The only thing breathing for Jade is that machine. Her heart could stop any time."

As Helga's lips moved silently in prayer, Tobin thought of Betts again and Jade saying, *If anything like that ever happens to me, I want to fly free.*

"We're losing her," Mr. Wellington said. He stood beside his wife, a quiet man. "There's no brain wave, no chance for her to get better. I never thought you could lose someone with asthma. But the doctor said they lose a few cases every year."

That evening Tobin was with the Wellingtons when Jade's heart quit beating. They collapsed into each other's arms. Tears ran down Helga's face as she turned back to her daughter and leaned over the rail. "I love you, dear child," she said, patting her face.

It was some minutes before Mr. Wellington murmured, "Tobin, could we talk to your father?"

She nodded. "He's out in the lobby with Jon. I'll stay here with Jade just a minute more."

He nodded his approval and then walked out hand in hand with his wife. Left alone with her best friend, Tobin leaned once more over the shiny rail and pressed her face against Jade's and whispered. "You told me we were born to fly free. You're free now, Jade. But I promise you, no matter how long it takes, I will find out who gave you that coffee. I won't rest until I know the truth.''

When she left the unit and went back to the lobby, Jon was waiting for her, his arms wide open. As she stepped into them, he pressed her cheek against his broad chest, and rested his chin on the top of her head.

''Where's Dad?'' she asked.

''In the chapel with the Wellingtons. They want your father to conduct the funeral service.''

She pulled away and rebelled openly. ''Not my father. How could he speak for my friend? He didn't really know her.'' In a boldness that was not her own, she said, ''I will speak for my friend. I'm telling you, Jon, the church may not have been there when Jade Wellington moved among us, but they'd better be there to tell her goodbye.''

His eyes misted. ''They'll come in droves, straight out of the woodwork. I promise you, sweetheart, the church will be packed out.''

She cried and sputtered, ''Jade would laugh at that. But then, friends should stick closer than brothers. Jade did. I've known her for such a short while, but it feels more like forever.''

''She was that kind of person.''

''I'll tell her friends that nothing could pluck Jade Wellington from God's hand, not even that tainted cup of coffee. I'll tell them about Running Springs and make them laugh when I describe her climbing down from the upper bunk and putting her bare foot in my face.''

''That's the way we want to remember her, Tobby. Bursting with energy. Making people laugh.''

''I'll make them cry, too,'' Tobin said. ''She was wheezing that day, Jon, but she was stepping out into the night to check God out.'' Her voice wavered. ''Lately she's been telling me that she was slow of heart like the men on the Emmaus Road, but I have no doubt that on this final leg of the journey, her Savior walked and talked with her through the valley.''

''Even here in the hospital?'' Jon asked. ''If so, maybe this God of yours allowed these last few days between deep coma and eternity to allow us time to say goodbye, to accept that she was going.''

His arm was around her as they began the long walk down the corridor toward the glass doors. ''Jon, a few moments ago Jade reached the end of her Emmaus Road. And I believe Someone up there said, 'Do you see me now? I've been here all along. Come along, I will give you rest.' And Jade just stepped into His outstretched arms.''

From the corner of her eye, she saw Jon smile. ''Your message is getting to me, sweetheart. I think your father better put away his sermon notes right now. He won't be needing them.''

In the distance, the doleful chimes in the university towers rang out. For a second, Tobin's face twisted. ''Jade should be heading for her history class if she—''

''No regrets, Tobby. Jade is in a far better place now.''

Chapter Seventeen

Late Christmas afternoon the Michelsons and their guests gathered around the piano to sing Christmas carols. The music stuck in Tobin's throat. How could anyone sing in this season of grieving? Her best friends were gone—Jade out of reach and Jon on the freeway driving back from his sister's home in San Diego.

Tobin left the room and found Gramps in the kitchen nibbling another slice of turkey. "You're not staying for the evening?" she asked.

"Got a paper to run."

"But, Gramps, it's Christmas."

"You'd be one of the first ones fussing if the paper didn't appear at your doorstep in the morning." He cupped her chin with turkey bits still on his fingers. "You all right, my girl?"

"I'll be okay."

'If there's anything I can do…''

"I'll call you." She began packing a basket of food.

"None for me," he said. "Can't stand leftovers."

"I'm making a house call."

"The Wellingtons?" His bushy brows cruised up and down. "You have to let what happened go."

"Not until I know what really happened. If I don't, people are going to end up saying Jade committed suicide."

"We know better than that. That girl was a champion. She never took the escape route."

"Then you've got to help me prove it."

He groused, "I won't use my paper to make a saint out of her."

"But if I find the truth, will you print it?"

He brushed the crumbs from his rotund belly. "You give me a newsworthy story, Tobby, and I'll print it."

Tobin drove to the Wellingtons with platters of turkey and dressing and the pie her mother had baked for them. The weather was chilly enough, but she felt cold inside as she rang the bell. Tears pricked her eyes at the thought of Jade bursting through the door, shouting, "I'm home."

Yes, Jade was Home.

Helga Wellington opened the door, her face drawn and tired. "Tobin, what are you doing here on Christmas Day?"

"I was afraid you'd be alone."

"We are. Mike went to his in-laws. They thought it would be a happier place for the children."

Tobin held up the basket. "I brought your dinner—

turkey and all the trimmings. We just have to warm it up in your oven.''

Helga rubbed her arthritic knuckles. "I haven't eaten much lately, but dear Paul could do with a decent meal.''

There was a quiet dignity to Jade's parents as they welcomed her, and though they sat together and talked for an hour in the kitchen, none of them could find the courage to speak of Jade.

"Has Jon come by to see you?''

"We thought you would come by together." Helga's words were tempered with kindness. Her eyes—so much like Jade's—brightened for a moment. "You love him, don't you, Tobin? You're not letting...what happened keep you apart, are you?''

Tobin looked away. "I need some time alone.''

"But loving includes being with each other when you're hurting." She took her husband's hand and allowed Paul's fingers to lock with hers. "Jon is family here.''

"Then he should be spending the time with you.''

"Losing Jenna several years ago was hard on him. But what happened to us ten days ago was almost more than Jon can bear. He watched...Jade grow up. Thought of her as his kid sister.''

"Then why isn't he here with you today?''

"He offered to take us to dinner. When we refused he said he'd take his presents down to his sister's. He'll be here this afternoon to watch the ballgame with Paul." She sighed wearily. "And he's coming all day New Year's to watch the games with Paul.

With Jon here, I can finish clearing out my daughter's apartment."

"Oh, not on a holiday."

"My dear, holidays don't mean much to me right now."

"I could help you. It might be easier with two of us."

"Oh, would you? I've dreaded going alone. Paul can't face it. We'll come back afterward and have supper with the men."

Tobin's cheeks flushed. "Jon will think I barged in."

She shook her head, her voice agitated. "I'm going to shake both of you. You will come back with me. Is that understood?"

"I could buy a chocolate or berry pie. Jon's favorites."

Helga smiled. "Jon likes home-baked pies. Why don't we bake the pies together? Jade and I used to do that. We had such fun—" She turned away quickly to hide her tears, then said, "Tobin, would you like something of Jade's to remember her by?"

"I won't forget her."

"But something tangible. Something you can hold on to."

Tobin thought about the diary. Did they know about it? Her suggestion to take Jade's key and search the apartment while Jade still lay in a coma had been met with Jon's angry rebuke. "We'll do no such thing," he had said, taking the key from her. "That's up to Paul and Helga."

But she had made a promise to her dying friend

and wanted to keep it. What happened might be in her diary. "I loved her grandmother's quilt. We used to sit on it and talk for hours."

"It's lovely, isn't it? My mother made one for Paul and me, too. The other day when we went by my daughter's apartment we picked up some of the things she really treasured. Her china cups and saucers. Her pictures. We looked for her emerald necklace, but didn't find it... But we did bring the quilt. I'm certain of that. It's in a box out in the utility room."

Helga led Tobin into the dankness of the workroom, past the washer and dryer to the built-in shelves on the back wall. Wind from the garage whipped beneath the door as she tugged down a box from the top shelf. She shivered. "It's this one, I believe. Yes, Paul marked it bedding." She carried the carton to the dryer and placed it on top. "Take it before I change my mind."

"If you do, I can bring it back...."

Tobin felt the soft coverlet and then as Helga walked away, she pressed deeply into the box until her fingers found the shape of the diary. So they didn't know it was there! She closed the box and hoisted it into her hands and left.

That night she took Jade's soft velvet-covered journal from its hiding place and sensed Jade's presence as she read it. Each day had its own page, filled to overflowing in Jade's neat penmanship. Parts of the diary were funny. Tobin remembered that wonderful rippling laughter of being with Jade. But the diary was like Jade's mood, swinging on a pendulum, back and forth. She choked on some of Jade's words, pondered on others and cried when she came to the last notations.

I saw Tobin today. Mike thinks we act like a couple of kids whenever we're together. That's what we were when we first met at Running Springs. When we met again, it was as though no time had passed between us. We clicked. We understood each other. She's smarter than I am, but I know people better. Tobby knows about bugs and migratory birds and names the sea turtles at her lab. I know people. I know what makes them tick. What makes them hurt.

Some of Tobin's knowledge is slowly rubbing off on me. But I think some of me—some of my love for other people—is reaching Tobin. She's coming out of the shelter of her church, and before long she's going to know what she really believes and stands for.

Jade's thoughts tended to merge, to ramble back and forth from one topic to the other. But over and over Tobin saw Jade's love for her family. Her love for Jon.

How wonderful to have a family like mine. Mike and Jon worry about me. I tell them everything's okay. As soon as the swim team wins the championship, I'll take my future seriously like Tobin does. Jon says I could go places with my photography. I'm going to ask for a new camera for Christmas. Cory smashed my old one.

Cory had smashed more than a camera. He had struck at the core of a person, but Jade had survived the onslaught and had come up stronger for it. Several pages later Jade had written:

Betts died this week after six years in a coma. I never want to be trapped like she was. Now I think of her flying free—or whatever you do after you die. Jon loaned me the money so I could send a dozen red roses. Dear God, how Betts loved red roses!

And then:

Kedrick's drinking is getting worse. He is determined to shame his father at the church. He is trying to persuade the young people to drink. He thinks it's cool. But he knows it could ruin his dad. If I told, no one would believe me. And if they believed me, Pastor Michelson might lose his job. I don't want to lose Tobin's friendship. With Betts gone, Tobin is my dearest friend. I'd rather die than hurt my friend.

On one of the last pages, it said, "I cried myself to sleep last night. I know Jon and Tobin are going to marry someday. They are such dear friends, but they haven't a clue how much Jon once meant to me." In the same paragraph, Jade wrote, "Kip was here with Kedrick. Tobin trusts Kedrick too much.

Maybe it's because they're twins. Today I told Tobin about my diary. I have a funny feeling that she'll be reading it soon. Life is strange. It's like my marriage. I thought that would go on forever, too.

In tiny print on the day before her death, Jade had written five phone numbers, five unidentified listings at the bottom of the page. "Someday Tobin will know what to do with these."

Tobin remembered the emergency room and Brent Carlson flipping open a tiny notebook with five phone numbers. She had copied them in the back of her checkbook and compared them now. They were the same five nameless numbers.

In January Tobin plunged into the new semester, burying herself in her books, determined to finish her course and move away from Auburn forever. She could function intellectually. She always had. She was dead emotionally. Even after spending New Year's Day with Jon at the Wellingtons', she kept making excuses when he called, refusing to go out with him. And on the weekends she could muster no enthusiasm for scaling the mountains.

How do you scale a mountain when you're wallowing in the valley? she asked herself.

Somehow she had made it through the past month. Now if she didn't pore over her reports on the *SeaGull* or continue her detailed notes on the environmental changes along the coastline, she would come unsoldered. Sheer willpower held her together.

As she opened the thick research volume in front of her, a Christmas tag fell from its pages. She pushed it aside as though it were venomous. How had she survived the holidays—decorating a tree smelling of pine needles, attending church functions, spending time with the Wellingtons. Over and over she'd read Jade's diary. Over and over she'd looked at the five phone numbers. The answers were there, but she had not found them.

On the coldest day in January, Tobin arose with the dawn and dressed warmly in her corduroy slacks and a snug wool jacket. She stuffed index cards and pens and a candy bar into her pockets. And then, tying her long hair back with a bright green ribbon that matched the leaf pattern in her jacket, she set out alone, driving through the early-morning mist to the ocean.

She parked on a side street because she didn't have enough quarters to feed the meter. The streets were empty as she crossed them and made her way to the beach. But the ocean was awake and she was drawn to it as the water crashed into a blowhole and sprayed its fury above her. She wandered aimlessly beside the surf, blinked against the sand blowing into her face. She picked up empty seashells and examined them, pocketing three of them to take back to her mother. Later, when she found a sheltered cove, she watched the sunlight change the color of the sea to amber, the tide wash out, the waves foam the shoreline.

She crouched by a tidal pool that looked much like a rocky bathtub filled with the wonders of nature. Snails grazed on the rocks, their rough-ribbed tongues feasting on plant life. She spotted a starfish with its bumpy arms, algae that felt like velvet and a limpet shell that reminded her of a Chinese hat.

When the high tide rolled in again, the rocky tub would become part of the ocean, its tiny inhabitants clinging to the rocks, and she would be forced to move back farther on the beach to safety. She gloried in being alone, knowing that what she knew to be tears would be considered by anyone passing her as the ocean splashing her face.

Jon found her there three hours later. His laced tennis shoes were thrown over one shoulder, his sweater sleeves and pant legs rolled up, his jacket tied around his waist. Wind and ocean spray had tousled his hair as though he had just stepped from the shower.

"Jon, how did you find me?"

"Your mother said you went to the ocean."

"But it's a big ocean."

He smiled ruefully. "I've been marching up and down this beach in segments for forty-five minutes. I figured you'd have your nose in a book, a pen in your hand."

"No book. But I brought something to write on and a candy bar that I'll share with you."

"Good, I'm famished. I started out by the rocks to look for you. I figured you'd be sheltered there studying the sea lions."

"I'm into pilot whales this week," she said lightly.

"A bit off season, isn't it?"

He dropped down beside her and brushed the sand from his hands. "But I knew you wouldn't be far from a tide pool."

"What makes you say that?"

"Remember our first walk on the beach?"

She blushed. "I'd forgotten. I was telling you all about the ecosystem and the seaweed jungle on the edge of the ocean."

"And about mussels and periwinkles—I always thought that was the color of your mother's apron. And about barnacles and limpets. And I didn't have a clue what you were talking about."

"And I didn't realize that until I looked up into your face. You looked so blank, Jon. So utterly bewildered."

"I was trying to look interested. But I learned a few things that day. Beach bugs hop. Seabirds fly. And that you were very beautiful, like you are now."

She brushed the loose strands of her windblown hair back from her face. "I'm a mess right now."

"Why did you come down here alone, Tobby?"

"To sort out my feelings about Auburn—and you. About all that's happened these last few weeks."

"Losing Jade shouldn't change our feelings for each other."

"I just need time, Jon."

"I need you. Why don't you return my phone calls?"

"I don't have to—you're here with me."

He scrambled to his feet and extended his hand. "Then walk with me," he said.

They left their shoes in the cove and started off, barefoot along the ocean. The water was cold as ice as it lapped their feet. She paused inland by another miniature sea world brimming with life. "Jon, I've been reading Jade's diary."

Their eyes met as he took her hand again. "You shouldn't read another person's secrets."

"I promised that I would one day. On one of the last pages, I found the same five phone numbers that we found in her purse."

"And you dialed them all?"

"Only the third number on the list," she said sadly. "It turned out to be the payphone at your boarding house."

"I never call you from the pay phone," he said. "What about the other four numbers?"

She felt his fury. "I haven't tried them yet, Jon."

"But you've drawn your own conclusions? You think I was the last person to see Jade before she reached the parsonage?"

"Were you, Jon?" she asked anxiously.

He released her hand, his face furious as he spun around and walked back over the beach toward their cars. She stood there watching him go, ashamed of what she had said, grieved that she had even suspected him for a moment. What was wrong with her? She loved him and had let him go. Accused him of something awful—unspeakable. She cupped her hands to call him back, but he was already gone, hidden by the sand dunes.

Chapter Eighteen

In mid-March, Tobin was sitting in the library with her books spread out in front of her when she heard the familiar tread of Jon's footsteps coming across the carpeted room. She looked up in surprise and smiled at him. For the past month and a half he had sent roses weekly—apologizing with the first bouquet for walking away from her on the beach, and telling her with each subsequent card how much he loved her. But he had not called.

Jon closed her books and pushed the research volumes aside. "The librarian can shelve them later." He pulled back her chair and took her hand. "Come," he whispered, "I want to talk to you."

Outside, he said, "Honey, it's one thing to respect the memory of a friend, to be loyal to Jade, but you can't shut the rest of us out. Your family and I need you."

He led her to his car. "We'll pick your car up later, Tobin. Right now we have an appointment down at the *City Herald* with your grandfather and Gilbert Gaspian.''

"The philanthropist? What does he want?"

"You'll see."

They rode the rest of the way with a smile tugging at Jon's lips. "I've missed you, Tobin. Missed being with you."

He held her hand as they walked into her grandfather's office. Gramps blew her a kiss. "About time you two got back together," he said. "Did you use force, Jon?"

Laughing, Gilbert Gaspian rose to shake her hand. "So this is the young woman who has been causing us all such grief?"

He was a stately gentleman, easily recognized on the streets of Auburn, a congenial man with a smile on his face and money to spend in any way he wanted. "Your grandfather and I go back a long way. K.T. and I met during the Korean War. We were luckier than some of our buddies, coming out unscathed."

"Since then he made his millions in banking investments," Gramps informed her. "I help him find ways to spend it."

"Yes, your grandfather draws up the plans. I pay for them." He was still smiling. "Now K.T. and I have teamed up again."

Gramps raised his bushy brows. "We're going to do follow-up editorials on Jade Wellington's influence on the swim team. We're going to inspire them to go on without her and win for her."

"We plan to squelch the rumors about suicide," Jon said.

Gilbert Gaspian seemed to be enjoying himself. "Your grandfather has written the first three editorials. One on the risks of becoming a champion. Another on overcoming obstacles like Jade did with her asthma. One on what happens when someone cuts that career short. We're promising our readers that we are going to prove that someone gave her that cup of coffee. And when we find him, we are going to spread that name across the front page."

"It might work," Tobin said hopefully. "But I don't understand how you are involved, Mr. Gaspian."

"We couldn't take you into our confidence earlier because I've been drawing up plans for a new park out beyond the gymnasium," he said, mischief in his eyes. "We're going to call this Jade Park so the town will rally behind us."

There was restraint in Jon's smile. "Someone here in Auburn won't want to pick up the paper these next few weeks. Someone else may remember who was with Jade at the café that night."

"This grandfather of yours is playing church," Gaspian said with a twinkle. "He's turning the paper into a confessional and using the park as a reward for future champions in this city."

Gramps said, "Tobby, we want Jade's life to inspire young athletes. Then we can put this tragedy to rest. We'll end with the announcement that Gilbert here is funding Jade Park for the young people of Auburn."

"No, Gramps, we'll end when we have the truth

and clear Jade's name. But I think your plan is going to work."

Back at Tobin's car, Jon said, "Tobby, I have new pictures of Angelo. Why don't you follow me home and come up to see them?"

"But what would Biddy think?"

"She knows you now. She'll understand."

"For a few minutes, then."

She had forgotten how narrow the steps were up to the attic apartment. She trudged on ahead of Jon and collapsed onto his daybed the minute she got there. The pictures were lying in a neat pile on his end table. She picked them up and began sorting through them. "He is such a good-looking little fellow. He has a personality all his own. I see it in his eyes."

Jon laughed. "What you see is a mischievous little boy who uses his eyes to get his way. Be wary of him when you meet him."

"Will I meet him?"

He eased down beside her. "That's still in the plans, isn't it? You. Me. Angelo."

As she looked at the snapshots again, something maternal tugged at her heart. She wanted to see him, to know him. But lately there had been no talk of marriage. Nothing about their future. The thought of having a life together had died with Jade.

Still she said, "I wish he were here in America so we could start doing things together."

Jon ran his hand the length of her arm, rubbing it gently. "Tobby, we've never talked about it. But you do want children, don't you?"

"I never made it a priority." Not until I met you, she thought. "I've been getting my education, preparing for a job."

"A career lady," he said sadly. "I would want my wife to stay at home."

She stacked the pictures together and placed them on the end table. "Mother did that. She's been content with nothing more."

"And you want more?"

"I've never understood how she could be happy with no profession of her own. I want my independence. Money in the bank. A chance to make my own decisions."

"Tobin," he said patiently, weighing his words, "I respect how far you've gone in your profession. But Angelo is going to need a stay-at-home mom."

"Is that negotiable?" she asked.

His serious smile clouded even more. "You have to understand, Tobin, what Angelo has been through. He's unsettled enough as it is. I can't ask him to accept a mother who juggles her time between the home and a research lab."

She leaned across and put her finger to his lips. "We're quarreling, Jon."

"No, we're not."

"We will be soon."

"We don't have time to fight, Tobin. We hardly see each other anymore."

"I've had things on my mind."

"I've tried to work around that. That's why we came up with that idea at the paper. But you worry about what Jade wrote in her diary. You worry about what's become of her necklace."

"Somehow I feel responsible for those things. Helga and I went through every nook and cranny in Jade's apartment. We looked in every box and drawer. Jade's emerald necklace was not there."

Jon licked his lip. "Is it so important to find it?"

"Yes, it belonged to her grandmother. Jade told me the chain had broken. I think she was having it repaired, but there was no jewelry stub or claim check in her apartment. So where is it?"

"Why do you ask me?"

"Because you're my rock. I share things with you, Jon. I feel wretched thinking one of her friends might have stolen it."

He ran his finger over the pattern on the cushion. "I thought you liked Kip and Casey."

"I do. They turned out to be real bricks. Helga would have given them something to remember Jade by if they'd asked her."

He looked at her and said helplessly, "You're right. They're not the kind to take something that doesn't belong to them." He forced her to look at him. "I have the necklace, Tobby. Jade gave it to me the night of the party."

"Then why did you wait so long to tell me?"

"After what happened? I couldn't find the right moment, not without you thinking I was the last one to see her."

Comprehending, she whispered, "Then you were with her. You're not the one she met at Knightbridge Café?"

"No, I went to her apartment before that."

He walked to his dresser and opened the top drawer, his back to her. She noted his finely shaped head. His broad shoulders. He stood there for several seconds and then retrieved a cloth-covered object and turned back to her, his mouth twitching.

"Her mother called me that night—told me to stay away from Jade. I headed right over to ask Jade what I had done wrong."

His mouth kept twitching. "Jade and I could always talk things over. But that night—"

"Jade was in love with you, wasn't she, Jon?"

He looked utterly miserable, as though he were betraying Jade. "She thought she was. She said she was going to transfer schools. I begged her not to go. I would have left town first."

"What must she have thought of me talking constantly about you. About our getting married one day and moving to Europe."

"She was that kind of a person. Willing to share your joy."

"But it must have hurt every time I did. I even made her promise that she'd stand up for me when we got married. Is that why she talked of transferring to another university?"

He moved back across the room to her. "Whatever troubled her that night, Jade wanted you to have her necklace. She said every bride wore something borrowed."

Slowly he unraveled the cloth and held the emerald up. It sparkled as it dangled in the light. "But it wasn't on loan. Jade intended for you to keep it because you admired it. She said she wouldn't need it any longer.''

"Oh, Jon, did she plan to die?''

"Jade was stronger than that. She was careful about her medical history and avoided anything that might set her asthma off. She would never have taken something deliberately.''

"Then what happened that night?''

His voice held steady as he said, "Jade's phone rang while I was still there in her apartment. I heard her make an appointment with someone at the café. Someone she knew. She was upset. Really angry—so angry she almost forgot I was still in the room.''

"Who was it?''

"I would only be guessing—but I think we both know.''

He slipped the necklace around her neck and turned her to face his mirror. He stood behind her. "It looks lovely on you.''

"But I can't keep it, Jon. I must give it back to Helga.''

"No, I talked to the Wellingtons last evening. I told them what happened. They insist that you keep it.''

They faced each other as the minutes ticked away. "I'm going back to Europe at the end of June. I want you to go with me as my wife.''

"You haven't even asked me to marry you. Not officially.''

"I asked your father some time back. I told him I planned to give you a ring at Christmas. And then— then with all that happened, it didn't seem right.''

"Jon, I can't leave in June. Not with so much still unsettled. Kedrick is drinking more than ever."

He ran his fingers over the back of her hand. "Maybe his problem is deeper than alcohol."

"I don't know. He won't talk about it. Jade's death tore him apart. I really think he was in love with her, Jon."

"Kedrick is not emotionally strong enough to love anyone right now. But I'm not asking Kedrick or your family to marry me. I'm asking you to be my wife, Tobby."

"Or are you asking me to be Angelo's full-time mother?"

She had stunned him again. "I want you both," he said. "We'll work something out, Tobin. I know how much your career means to you. I promise you, we'll work something out."

"Will we?" She touched the emerald. "Maybe I'd be afraid to trust you again. You knew I was looking for this—"

He turned on her so abruptly that it startled her. "Don't you realize I held back the truth to keep from hurting you? Yes, I had Jade's necklace. But I never betrayed Jade. I would never give her something that would cause her death."

She looked up into his face. "I know you better than that. I just wish I knew who did." She gripped the lapels of his jacket. "What happened is still tearing me apart."

He freed her hands and held them. "What's tearing you apart, Tobby, is not facing what really happened. You have all the puzzle pieces in your hand."

"You're holding my hands."

"Just to steady you. But begin to put the pieces together, Tobby, before your grandfather prints those editorials. I can't do it for you. The only way you'll find peace of mind again is to take out Jade's diary and dial those five numbers."

"You don't know what you're asking."

"But I do. You have to make the decision, Tobby. But just remember, I'm always here for you."

She tried to read the deep concern in his eyes. An ache bigger than life formed inside at the thought of him leaving Auburn. "But you're going away in June."

"I want you to go with me. I'm afraid of losing you if I fly back without you."

"Does Gramps know you're leaving?"

"Yes. I told him the other day. Old K.T. is rooting for the two of us. He wants you to run away with me."

"He would." She tried to smile, to make this moment light, bearable. "He hand-picked you for me the day he met you."

"From the moment I saw you, I didn't need his help. Tobin, there are only a few weeks left for you to make up your mind. I have to make reservations soon."

"Jon, I asked for an extension on my thesis. With all that's happened, the committee gave me until September. I can't think about getting married or moving away just yet."

"And I can't think about anything but us. But I can

wait. I'm as close as a phone call until the end of June. And then—'' His fingers locked with hers. ''Angelo and I will be as close as an international call.''

Chapter Nineteen

In April Tobin found the courage to look at the five phone numbers again. She crossed off the one to Jon's boardinghouse, then crossed off Wally's private number. Finally she drew a line through the fourth number, the one that had rung into Kip and Casey's studio. One number remained. She knew now that she had recognized it all along. She walked into her father's study and dialed.

"Hi," a familial voice said.

Her eyes teared. She started to replace the receiver when the man on the other end shouted, "Hello, who is this?"

"It's your sister, Kedrick. We have to talk."

"About you and lover boy Jon?" he slurred.

"About you and Jade—and the editorial Gramps wrote today."

He sucked in his breath. "You know where the stairs are."

"No, I want you to come up here. I'm in Dad's study."

As he slammed the receiver down, she sank into her father's leather chair, feeling small and insignificant sitting there. If she confronted Kedrick with the truth, it would ruin all of their lives. If she kept silent, it would betray the best friend she'd ever known.

Fifteen minutes later Kedrick came sulking into the room and sank into the chair opposite her. He had lost weight since Jade's death, the collar of his shirt hanging loosely around his neck.

"You know, don't you? How did you find out?" he asked.

She hadn't missed the belligerence in his voice. "Jade kept a diary—and Jon was in the apartment when you called her. Jon told me I'd figure it out one day. But I didn't want to face the truth. You're my brother and Jade my best friend."

His jaw pulsated. "I tried to give her a diamond that night, Tobby. And she turned me down. I wanted to take her to the birthday party and announce to everyone that we were engaged."

"But, Kedrick, the two of you never really dated."

"We were together all the time. I'd go over to her house to see her. Just to talk or for a haircut. I never missed her swim meets. I was with her every minute I could be." His lip curled. "And you know what she told me, sis? She told me she wanted to help me. That's why she was my friend. I loved her...."

Tobin ached for his humiliation. Ached because he really didn't know what love was all about.

"Dad came between us. He ruined it for me."

"It was Jade who rejected you, not Dad. Jade saw you for what you really are. Dad sees you for what he wants you to be."

"I can't live up to the family image. I never wanted to be a fifth-generation pastor. And, sis, I don't want to take over the paper. I want to get out of this town like you did."

"What happened between us, Ked? We were such good friends."

His eyes remained hostile. "Have I lost you, too, Tobby?"

"Never. I love you too much for that."

"All my life I played second fiddle to you. Everything you did succeeded." His eyes glazed. "All I really wanted was Jade."

"Ked, I want to know what happened that night."

"What good will knowing do? Jade is dead."

"I want to know why."

He gave her a helpless shrug. "I told her that I was going to drink myself into a stupor if she didn't meet me before the party. I was kidding, but I knew that would get her down to Knightbridge's. That's where I showed her the ring."

"In that crowded place?"

"She'd been there with me before. When she got up to leave, she said something about getting a coffee to go." He looked sly, still ready to worm his way out of the mess he was in. "She must have dropped the medication in her coffee."

"Jade took her coffee black. What happened, Ked? The truth."

His expression hardened. "She was in the pits so

I offered her something. Nothing dangerous. Just something to give her a boost for the party. She deserved it. She rejected me, Tobby. Me!''

His words ran together. "She turned my ring down. Made a fool of me, and there she was looking at me as though I were scum for even offering her something to lift her spirits. I wanted to make her look crazy at the party so I got her coffee and dumped the pills in it. I figured I'd have the last laugh.''

Tobin didn't move. "Jade never laughed again, Kedrick.''

His face twisted. "I didn't know she'd have an allergic reaction. I never meant to hurt her. You have to believe me. I've been trying to live with myself ever since she died.''

Drinking yourself into a stupor, she thought. Withdrawing from everyone. "Kedrick, why didn't you tell us the truth right away? If the doctors had known sooner—''

"Don't hang me with that one, sis. And don't tell anyone. It's over now. It won't help anyone to know what happened.''

"It will salvage Jade's reputation. And it might help you.''

"Tobin, if you turn me in, it will ruin Dad.''

"And if I don't, it will ruin you.''

"I could go to prison, Tobby. I—''

A deep masculine voice interjected, "Would it be any worse than the prison you've been in these last few months, son?''

Kedrick stumbled from his chair and spun around to face his father. Ross looked as ashen as his son.

Slowly he came into the room, his sorrowful gaze meeting his daughter's.

His gaze settled back on Kedrick. "Forgive me for failing you, son." His hands trembled. "But I want to help you now. We'll have to talk to Brent Carlson—and to the Wellingtons."

"And to the deacon board?" Kedrick asked bitterly.

"No, son. This is a family matter."

A dreadful silence swept over the room. At last Kedrick took the first halting step toward his father. Ross met him halfway.

"Son, I love you."

"I know," Kedrick answered, his face crushed against his father's shoulder. "You have always loved me."

Tobin left and closed the study door behind her, praying that Kedrick would find his way to peace. Fleetingly she thought, *Dad may have to resign from the pastorate. The deacons may give him no choice. But Dad will stand with my brother.*

An hour later Tobin stood by Jade's grave, running her hands over the shiny marble marker. Her eyes blurred as she read, "Our Jade, Our Jewel." The hummingbird and butterflies on the marker were in flight, their wings spread. "Jade," she cried to the emptiness, "I promised you I wouldn't give up until I knew what happened. I know now, but there's no satisfaction in knowing."

A refreshing spring wind cut across the cemetery. A half hour passed, then she stood slowly. "I'm finally free to let you go. I'll see you again," she whispered. "Not here, but in heaven. No one, not even Kedrick's foolishness, could pluck you from God's hand. Please forgive Kedrick. He didn't mean to destroy you."

As Tobin retraced her steps over the grassy hillside, the afternoon breeze brushed against her tears. Above her a bird balanced on the tree limb, twittering, making melody in its breast. She watched, enthralled.

Birds can always sing, she thought. Why can't I?

The bird winged heavenward where frothy clouds floated lazily across the blue sky; they stretched out like God's canopy over the cemetery—over Jade. Suddenly a glimmering, shimmering path of sunlight split through the blue. Unexpected peace filled Tobin. She didn't know what would happen to Kedrick, but she knew Jade would want mercy.

As she neared the cemetery gate, she saw Jon coming to meet her. They stopped at the same time. Above the grave markers their eyes met. "Oh, can you forgive me, Jon, for doubting you? I thought—"

"You know, then?" he asked calmly. "What about Kedrick?"

"Kedrick is turning himself in." The wind caught her words and blew them toward Jon. "Dad went with him. But how did you know it was Kedrick, Jon?"

"It had to be. I knew Jade was meeting someone at the café. Kip and Casey were already at the party. Kedrick never showed up. No one at the café could remember—or would remember—who was there with

Jade that night. I'd heard Jade on the phone, agreeing to meet someone. I knew it had to be Kendrick.''

"Oh, Jon, how can you ever forgive me?"

"Because I love you. Because I never stopped loving you."

She marveled at his steady, unblinking gaze. He took a step toward her, his arms open. "Tobin, you know I'll stand by you and your family."

She nodded gratefully. "I called Brent Carlson before coming to the cemetery. He said no charges were ever filed."

"I talked to Brent, too, Tobby. He said Jade's case is open-ended. They can't nail Kedrick on his drinking this time, but Carlson is still hoping that Judge Nanry will insist on him entering a recovery program. He said the best we can hope for is that the records will stand—an accidental death."

Tobin chewed her lower lip. "I don't want to think about the alternative. Not yet. But all his life, Kedrick stood in the shadows—second fiddle to me, he always told me. I never could see it until Jade died. Now I know what he meant. Gramps and Dad pushed him to succeed. He kept falling short of their demands."

"Kedrick made his own choices."

"He was always in trouble. I used to cover for him, not wanting them to know how weak he really was. That's why I moved away for five years. That's why I dreaded coming back."

He put his arms around her. "If you hadn't come back, Tobin, I would never have found you."

She nodded. "I thought if I defended him, he'd realize I was his friend. Now for the first time in our lives, I'm stepping out of the way. I'm going to let him face up to the truth.''

"When he does, his dad can really be proud of him."

"But at what a price." Tobin glanced back at Jade's grave. "Jade's death really got to Dad. He's reaching out to strangers in a way he never did before. And he's been praying that we'd find the one who gave Jade those pills. He's gone from wanting judgment to a yearning for that person to find peace."

"Never knowing that he was praying for his own son? What will this do to him, Tobin? Will Ross resign from his pulpit?"

"Most likely, he will want to relinquish his position with the church and do everything he can for his son. Mother will agree."

"They'll come through," Jon said. "Kedrick loved Jade in his own way. I think he's genuinely sorry for what happened."

"I know, but he doesn't understand forgiveness."

Jon brushed tear-wet strands of hair from her face. "I've learned that confession comes first, Tobby. When Jade died, I wanted nothing to do with that God of yours. And then you spoke so lovingly at the funeral about a friend sticking closer than a brother. And it blew my mind when you said that nothing could pluck Jade from God's hand. It helped the Wellingtons, too."

Her heart was still heavy, yet strangely enough her heartbeat was beginning to do flip-flops in Jon's presence. His chin rested on top of her windblown hair. "Tobby, for what it's worth, it helped me make my own decision about walking with God. Even when you doubted me, my commitment to Christ was genuine. I knew that no matter what happened between us, nothing could pluck me from God's hand. I was His on a permanent basis. Like Jade was."

His voice grew husky. "I love you, Tobby."

Impulsively he leaned down and tenderly kissed her there in the cemetery. The crinkle lines around his eyes relaxed as she drew away, but his gaze still engulfed her, adored her. "It'll work out," he said gently. "I'll be there with you through an investigation. We'll reach out to Kedrick together. That's the way Jade would want it."

"But I'm afraid what the courts will do."

"We can't outguess them. We'll have to wait and see. Kedrick never intended to harm her. It wasn't something he bought illegally. Just an over-the-counter medication. *But he did mix it in her coffee.*"

"Jon, we need to tell my grandfather and the Wellingtons before they hear it from someone else."

They turned, arms around each other, and walked to Jon's car. Tobin's spirits soared. The long nightmare was ending. As Jon helped her into the car, she grasped his hand and held it against her cheek. "I love you, Jon Woodward."

Smiling, he leaned down and kissed her again.

Gramps rubbed his hand vigorously and then, ignoring his computer, rolled a sheet of paper into his well-worn typewriter.

"You don't have to do the editorial this time,

Gramps. Let it go. You've done so much for Jade already."

"I promised this town that the *City Herald* would do all it could to preserve Jade's reputation. I promised you that we would not say goodbye to your friend without clearing her name and seeking judgment on the one who caused her death."

"But that was before we knew..."

His fingers hit the keys. Tears stole down his ruddy cheeks. She peered over his shoulder and read the words as he typed them.

"Our town planned to go to the national competitions with Miss Wellington splashing her way to victory for Auburn. We have known for some time that someone cut that dream short."

He wrote of the risks she took. The obstacles she overcame. About the team stirred to go on to win for her. He was banging out a fourth paragraph. "I have championed truth in the *Herald*. I have accepted nothing less and apologized when I was wrong."

In the last paragraph he crossed through several lines and settled on: "Today I am proud of my grandson, Kedrick Michelson. Our readers know him as one of our sports editors. They recognize the quality of his work. Today I urge you to recognize the quality of his confession. Today my grandson, my namesake, has begun his journey into manhood...."

He tore the sheet of paper from his typewriter. "Tobby, get this to one of my editors to run off on the computer for me. I need to leave..."

"But, Gramps, you have a paper to run."

"My staff can run the presses. They're dependable.

The newspaper will hit the stands on time. It always does," he bragged. "The townspeople depend on K. T. Reynolds!"

He took his jacket from the rack. "If you need me, Tobin, I'll be at the police station with my grandson."

"Do I have time to get to Jade's family and explain everything before they read about it in the paper?"

He glanced at his watch. "You'd best get a move on you."

Outside the newspaper office, Jon was waiting for her. He slipped his arm around her waist. "Where to next?" he asked.

"To the Wellingtons."

He opened the car door for her. "And after that?"

"To the park. Just the two of us."

"Why?" he asked candidly.

"So I can tell you how much I love you, Jon Woodward."

Later as they left the Wellingtons and drove slowly to the park, Tobby said, "Jade's family is so loving. So forgiving."

"Honey, I'm proud of what you just did. When you told them about Kedrick, you risked them filing charges. But they won't."

"I know." She stared out the window, watching reflectively as a jetliner flew off into the clouds. Then she began to laugh.

He reached for her hand. "Honey, what's wrong?"

"I'm all right, Jon. For the first time in months, I'm all right. I was just thinking about Jade. She always said we were meant to fly. Birds do. Planes do. We don't.''

He hunched down, studying the sky. ''We'd need wings.''

''Jon, have you ever done any hang gliding?''

''Once,'' he said guardedly.

''Would you teach me how?''

''I'd need more lessons myself.''

''I want to solo as soon as possible. I want to be up there soaring free. I want to know how Jade feels right now.''

He squeezed her hand. ''Jade feels totally free,'' he said.

Tobin's voice filled with excitement. ''Hang gliding will be about as close as I can come for now.''

''But I have to warn you, I frown on solo flying.'' He drove into the empty space at the park and pulled her to him. ''I've soloed through life long enough, Tobin. I want us to spend the rest of our lives together.'' Tenderly he tilted her chin toward him. ''When things settle down for Kedrick and your family—when you're up to it—let's go hang gliding on our honeymoon? Or catch a jet to somewhere special. To England, maybe?'' he teased.

''I'd like that, Jon,'' she said, lifting her mouth to his. ''I'd like that more than anything else in the world.''

Epilogue

Tobin stood on the golden, sun-drenched hills of the Cotswolds and watched her son race across the field kicking the soccer ball with his friends. Angelo was almost ten, but small for his age, his auburn hair tousled, his sturdy legs carrying him over the ground with lightning speed.

Angelo Woodward—their son now, Jon's and hers, with all the legality and paperwork of claiming him finally behind them. For two years she had watched him blossom. He still had Bosnian nightmares, but during the daylight, waking hours he was growing more confident. He no longer shrank away from strangers or ran at the sound of loud, banging noises.

Belonging to them had changed their frightened little boy into a happy one. Jon's assignments still took him throughout the continent on photo shoots, but for Angelo's sake they had chosen to make their home in the quiet of the Cotswolds. And Tobin had come slowly to the decision to limit her work schedule. She had taken on research projects for the university back home, and once a week she still traveled to London, keeping her career alive with a part-time position at the aquarium. Angelo saw her now as he sped back across the field, his laughter blending with that of the other children. He paused, waved and then ran to her.

She opened her arms and he fled there, lingering long enough for a quick hug and then backed away shyly. "The boys don't believe me, Mummy," he said.

"Don't believe you?"

"About the baby."

She patted her tummy. "They will soon. You're excited, aren't you, Angelo?"

He nodded, his face serious. "I don't know whether I ever had a sister. But maybe…"

She touched his cheek. "You will have one now."

His face lit with a brilliant smile. "Oh, there's Dad. I thought he was already off to London."

"Without saying goodbye to us? Not a chance."

"Will he be back tonight with—you know who?"

"He'll be gone a couple of days, then we'll all be together."

"Will your mum and dad like me?"

"They'll love you. You're their first grandchild."

He seemed pleased, but he toed the ground. "What will I call them?"

"I told you, darling. Gramps and Grammy. Or Grampa Ross—"

"Will they really like me?" he asked again.

"They'll love you."

Contented, he went with her to meet Jon, walking

side by side, inches apart, as close as forever. Tobin could not remember a time when she had been happier. Jon. Angelo. The baby.

She loved the rangy man coming toward her. Jon looked much as he had looked that first day she met him, with an unruly lock of dark hair cascading over his forehead and his thick brows arcing as he reached them. Jon with his handsome features and unblinking gaze. He had seemed striking to her that first day and still did—Jon, the university professor, as she had first known him, only happier, more suntanned. His skin seemed to absorb the golden hues of the Cotswolds. And here she was two years married and her heart was still doing flip-flops at the sight of him.

He tweaked Angelo's cheek affectionately and turned to her with a wink.

"You're not getting by with that," she said. Tugging at his tie, she pulled him toward her until his laughing lips found hers.

"Kiss me like that again," he said, "and we'll have to send someone else to Heathrow to pick up your parents."

"Will you be back tonight?" Angelo asked.

"No, son. I don't pick your mummy's parents up until midnight." He glanced over Angelo's head. "I've booked rooms at the Ritz."

"Jon, that's too expensive."

"It's just for one night. Your mom will love it. We'll be home in time for supper tomorrow. I'll give them a quick tour of London first, especially Westminster Abbey and the Holy Trinity in Kensington."

"Don't forget St. Paul's Cathedral. That's a must for Dad."

With a glance at his friends, Angelo said, "See you, Dad."

He went running back across the field. As they watched him, Jon put his arm around Tobby and drew her closer. "I never dreamed I could be so happy."

"I just wish Kedrick were coming with Mom and Dad."

"Someday, Tobby. Just be grateful they suspended his sentence so he could enter the recovery program. And once he finishes those two years of community service, I want him to join us for a while. I think he would enjoy photographing the Cotswolds. He could get back on his feet in a place like this."

He kissed her again, very gently. Then she walked him to the car, and when his car had slipped from view, she went back into the thatched house to write two letters, one to Gramps and one to the Wellingtons. Gramps had promised to come for a visit when the baby came, but Tobby was realistic. She was certain that they would have to go to him to show off the children. Gramps would never leave the newspaper office for a trip abroad.

She sealed his letter, smiling at the thought of him reading it, and then she took up her pen to write the more difficult letter. "Dear Helga and Paul," she began.

I know we haven't written for ages. And yet you are so dear to us, so very special. Jon especially feels this, with his own parents gone.

He says that you are his family, and he means it. We will never forget how kind you were to us, coming to our wedding so soon after losing Jade.

And you, Paul, coming to our rescue when Gramps sprained his ankle and had to hobble into the church on crutches. He had always planned to give me away—from the day he met Jon—and then he wasn't able to do so. Paul, you were so handsome in your Coast Guard uniform walking me down the aisle. I think of that often.

I can still hear you saying, "Your father can't be in two places at once, Tobin. Let me do the honor. I'll get you down that aisle and he can tie the knot."

Inside, I was crying, knowing that you were missing Jade so intensely. We both were. We both knew you would never be able to walk your own daughter down the aisle and give her away to someone as kindhearted and caring as Jon.

Can you believe, it has been two years already? Two years since we moved to England. Two fabulous years for Jon and me. Angelo is ours now. We can hardly believe our good fortune. We fought such hard battles in the courts and I think the barrister finally got tired of seeing us. So our little guy is Angelo Woodward now, such a handsome little fellow. We've included pictures so you can see for yourselves. Our little angel.

He has the brightest of dark brown eyes—woeful one minute, full of mischief the next. Jon is gone often on photo assignments, so we thought it best to settle in the village where Angelo has been so happy. People are so good to us here.

I think there is a bit of the biologist in Angelo. We go down by the river and spend hours there discovering the different algae and wee animals that live there. We've taken him to Cornwall twice and he seemed intrigued with tide pools. I told him it was an ocean in miniature.

Angelo still cries out in the night, and Jon goes in and holds him—or I do when Jon is gone. We cradle him as though he were still a small child—not almost ten. We hold him until the nightmare goes away. The doctor tells us that he will continue to have troubled sleep because it takes so long to erase the ravages of war. But he is having the nightmares less frequently now.

The doctor told us something else! And this more than anything has brought happiness to Angelo and to us. We have told him that he will have a sister soon and he can hardly wait. We wonder at times if he had a sister in his past, a young playmate in Bosnia. Of course, we will never know, but his new baby sister will join him in a few months.

Yes, our firstborn will be a girl.

And that is one reason I am writing. We want to call her Jade. We want to know if this will be all right with you, Paul and Helga?

I sit here even now at my small desk with Jade's emerald around my neck, my wedding jewel. I shall treasure it always. But I do not need jewelry to remind me of her.

She was, in that brief time of our friendship, the dearest of friends. She was as Jon said like a beautiful, fragile-winged butterfly, balanced on a tiny leaf, ready to take flight. At other times she was ready to take on the world and solve everybody's problems. Mine included. She was always there for me. If it had not been for Jade encouraging both of us, Jon and I would not be together, would not be enjoying this life together.

Thinking of it now—as I so often do—Jade lived as though tomorrow might not come. We understand why now. But mostly Jon and I think of her as flying free. The way she wanted to be. No longer earthbound as we all are, but totally free. Totally whole. We keep the photograph of her in the living room—her long blond hair blowing behind her, those vivid blue eyes honest and fair. If we miss her so dearly, what must it be for you? We pray often for you—for courage for each new day.

We will keep her picture always, because we will want our Jade—our little jewel—to know your Jade. We want our little girl to be part of your world. You will come to visit us, won't you? We'd like you to be part of her life—as your Jade was part of ours. We love you,

Tobin

Tobin had just finished the letter when Angelo

burst in through the door. She expected him to announce his hunger pangs. Instead he glanced at Jon's
picture on the end table and then leaned against her.
"I sure miss Dad," he said. "I like it when he's here
with us."

"Me, too. But he'll be back."

"Mum, I think I remember when I first saw him."

"Me, too," she said.

A tiny frown puckered his brow. "I think he just
picked me up and held me."

She laughed. "In a way, he picked me up, too, at
my grandfather's newspaper office."

"He must think we're very special."

"Oh, he does." Standing, she slipped her arm
around him. "Angelo, your father loves us both very
much."

* * * * *

Dear Friend,

Friendships come to us as one of life's treasures. Some friendships are momentary in time, others lifelong. Even the loss of a friend in death only deepens the remembered good times, the trust, the laughter, the way that friend stood with us through thick and thin, accepted us with all our flaws, gently pulled the reins when we strayed, cheered us when we were sad, rejoiced when we succeeded.

Recently a friend from the distant past traced my phone number and called to thank me for having touched her life long ago. The silent years vanished as though they had never been; the friendship budded again. And I reminded myself that I must thank my friends now for how much they have changed my life, how much they have blessed me.

Proverbs speaks of "a friend sticking closer than a brother," the words ringing with loyalty. The theme of friendship runs through *The Wedding Jewel.* Jade Wellington touches the lives of the hero and heroine, leaving them the richer for having known her, and allowing their own love to mushroom because of her sacrifices.

Dear reader, when you count your blessings, count your friends and be sure to count Christ among them.

In Friendship,

Doris Elaine Fell